S IS FOR SECOND CHANCE

ANNIE J. ROSE

Copyright © 2020 by Annie J. Rose

All rights reserved.

No part of this book may be reproduced in any form or by any electronic or mechanical means, including information storage and retrieval systems, without written permission from the author, except for the use of brief quotations in a book review.

This is a work of fiction. Names, characters, businesses, places, events and incidents are either the products of the author's imagination or used in a fictitious manner. Any resemblance to actual persons, living or dead, or actual events is purely coincidental.The following story contains mature themes, strong language and sexual situations. It is intended for mature readers only.

All characters are 18+ years of age and all sexual acts are consensual.

Photography: Wander Aguiar

DESCRIPTION

**I came in for the company's secrets.
I ended up making the boss my baby daddy.**

Devin was the mistake I hadn't counted on.
Three years ago, I went undercover to help my dad out.
He needed me to get intel on a rival company, so I posed as an intern.
My corporate spy mission went awry really quickly thanks to the boss's son, Devin.
Piercing blue eyes and sexy as hell, he was irresistible.
I was 19 and way in over my head.
Our hot, wild affair ended when I slipped away with company secrets.
Devin's been trying to destroy my dad's business ever since.
He's out for revenge.
If he knew about my little secret, he'd be furious, unstoppable.
She's two years old, my whole world.
Now my dad needs my help again, and I'm going into the lion's den.

I have to go toe-to-toe with the only man I ever loved, the man who set my body on fire and stole my heart.
Competing against him, wondering what trick he has next up his sleeve.
I don't trust him. But I want him.

And it's time to go back where I swore I'd never go.
With my heart and my secret on the line.

CHAPTER 1

DEVIN

Perfect. Everything was going absolutely fucking perfect. I was at the height of my career. The new launch was going off without a hitch. Everything was going exactly as it should, and yet, I was in a pissy mood. I moved through the crowd of men in tuxes, most of them owned and not rented. Women were wearing fancy gowns and dresses that showed off all their assets with their status of wealth obvious by the jewelry they wore. It was a real who's who in New York City with plenty of journalists to document every move.

This ballroom of one of the best hotels in the city had been decked out to exude elegance, class, and of course, wealth. Thousands of twinkle lights hung from the ceiling with iridescent gossamer draped over the walls, creating a shimmering effect. Catering staff milled around the room dressed in staunch white shirts with black slacks, each of them skilled professionals when it came to moving without really being seen.

The food was exquisite and the champagne freely flowing. No expense had been spared. We had set out to impress our colleagues, competition, and potential business partners. We had succeeded. I smiled and nodded as I moved through the crowd. I could mingle and schmooze with the best of them, but I had been doing it all night.

I needed a break. I needed a moment to breathe something other than cloying perfume and powerful cologne intermingling with the scent of the herbs coming from the appetizers being carried around on silver trays.

A flash went off, nearly blinding me and stopping me dead in my tracks. "Devin!" someone shouted. "Mr. McKay can I get a picture?"

I pasted on a fake smile and turned to my left to face the massive flash mounted atop a camera inches from my face. "I believe you just did," I said coolly before continuing on my way.

I wasn't being rude, but I had taken enough pictures over the last two hours to last me a lifetime. I was still seeing spots in front of my eyes. I had posed with all the movers and shakers in the industry. I had shaken hands while being photographed with fellow investment partners and kissed the cheek of damn near every woman in the gala while it was captured forever in a digital image.

Devin McKay had played his part.

I straightened the bow tie of my own tux as I scanned the crowd, noting every person in attendance and making mental notes about who had networked with whom. I was gathering intel, preparing for my next move. All of us were. It was why we all attended events like the one I was putting on.

I could feel the energy, and it was all positive, but it was doing nothing to ease the feeling that something wasn't quite right in my world. It was like someone running a cold fingertip down my spine. Nothing too ominous, but simply not right.

I knew what it was but I had been trying to ignore it. Tonight was one of the best nights of my life. The biggest product launch for my company was going off without a hitch. My right-hand man, Wes Brown, and his very creative and beautiful wife, Rian, had things well in hand. Their daughter Ronny was the life of the stuffy party. I had enjoyed chasing the little sprite around and even danced with her riding my feet for a few songs. It had been the highlight of my night.

Everything was perfect. I couldn't ask for things to go any better. Yet, there was that feeling that wouldn't go away. I knew what was causing the discomfort. I was having a crisis of conscience, and I didn't like it. I hadn't even done anything to deserve that feeling in my gut—yet.

Could I really pass up the chance to take down one of my biggest rivals? The man that had embarrassed the hell out of me and made me a disgrace to my father three years earlier. I had vowed revenge the moment my world crashed down around me and my heart was shattered at the hands of a woman who had set out to ruin me.

That wasn't something a man could just let go. There were sins to be answered for, and I was the one to make them pay. I *would* make them pay. But was I ready to pull the proverbial trigger?

"Hey," Wes said, stepping in front of me.

"Hey," I answered, my eyes still scanning the room.

"This should be one of the best nights of your life," he commented.

I offered my best smile. "It is. You guys outdid yourself."

"Then why do you look like you're waiting for an assassin to burst through the door?" he asked. "Look around you. You have no enemies here. Everyone is here to support you. Get something to eat."

"Why?"

"Because the fucking food is amazing and because you look constipated or something."

I rolled my eyes before clapping him on the shoulder. "I'm good. I was actually headed for the bar to get a drink. I think all the interviews are done for the night, and now it's time to relax and enjoy this thing."

"Good. I think Rian and I are going to make our escape soon. I don't want her feet swelling."

I smiled and nodded. Rian's pregnancy seemed to be going smoothly, but he was a very overprotective husband. "You're good to her. You two have a good night."

"See you later," he said and walked away.

I did head for the bar, ordered a double of my favorite whiskey, and carried the glass out to the balcony. I needed a minute to think. I needed to clear my head and weigh my options. I stepped onto the balcony, the sounds of the city at night filling my ears. I leaned against the rail, taking a long deep breath before blowing it out and taking the first drink of whiskey of the night.

I tried to stay stone-cold sober when I was at events like this. I couldn't afford to fuck up and say the wrong thing to the wrong person. I couldn't afford to make a move on a woman that was married to someone I needed to stay in good standing with. I had learned the hard way that women were cunning. They only wanted one thing from me—my company, which naturally includes my reputation and money.

I took another drink from the glass and let the liquid fire burn through my veins, falling into my gut and stoking the flame of revenge. I had worked three years for this very moment, and instead of pulling the trigger and making the move to destroy Ron Savage and his wily daughter, Elly, I was still fucking contemplating it.

I shook my head, trying to dissect the feelings I was having. Why the hell wasn't I jumping on the chance to steal the investment opportunity out from Savage? A little birdy had told me about the start-up that was quietly looking for a little cash. I had done my research and found out Savage was looking to get in on the deal. It was a Hail Mary for a company that was falling apart.

I could swoop in and steal it all right out from under him. It would be the final nail in the company's coffin. It would be the completion of a mission I had set out on three years ago. But I was hesitating because every time I thought of the Savage company going up in smoke, I remembered the prettiest pair of deep blue eyes.

I pulled my phone from my pocket, quickly unlocked it, and opened the file with the picture I looked at often. I stared at the image of the two of us together, my arm thrown around her shoulders. She had her face turned toward me, looking up at me with adoration. I remembered the moment the picture had been taken. We'd been out on the boat, both of us a little pink from the sun and our hair windblown. We'd had what I thought was one of the best days of my life.

It wasn't a week later when she walked out on me and took all the company secrets with her. She'd played me. She had played us all. She'd pretended to be an eager young intern, cozied up to me, a man older than her by fourteen years, and I fell for it. I fell for her innocent, wide-eyed stare like a damn fool.

She had fucked me over in every way, single-handedly ruining the biggest deal of my career at that time. She had pulled off subterfuge that would have impressed the top spies in the world. She had walked out the door with all my hard work and delivered it on a silver platter to her scheming father, but the fucking idiot couldn't even pull it off. I had done all the legwork, and he had still screwed it up.

He had destroyed the deal. The potential profits that could have been made for all concerned parties had gone up in smoke under his mismanagement. I not only had to deal with my father's disappointment, but my reputation had taken a hard hit. I had just finally managed to get my dad to give me the reigns to company, and I damn near lost it all on one deal gone wrong. Because of her.

Her betrayal still caused acid to burn in my belly. She had left me without a word. She didn't even bother to gloat. She'd just completely ghosted me, and from the moment I learned what she had done, I vowed revenge. For three long years I had systematically been dismantling the Savage investment firm. I was picking him off, one deal at a time.

I now held the final blow in my hand. I had come upon the information via some back channels I always kept open. It would be a sneak attack, just like he had dealt me. It was the coup de grace, the moment of victory I had craved.

"Don't be a little bitch," I cursed under my breath.

I was second-guessing my decision because of her. She certainly hadn't bothered to think about *my* feelings or what her actions would cost me. I shouldn't have given her a second thought. It showed my weakness.

I slid my thumb over the screen and pulled up my contact list. I pushed the button for one of the members that sat on the board of my company. I knew I could count on him to quietly carry out my orders.

"Tom," I said when he picked up the phone.

"Devin! How's it going? I figured you would be celebrating."

"I am, but I need you to do something."

"What's going on?" he asked, turning very serious.

"I've got some information about a start-up that is looking for some capital. It's a great opportunity. I'd like you to very discreetly make an offer. A generous offer. I'd rather not have this discussed with the board or anyone else just yet."

He cleared his throat. "I understand. Send me the information and I'll take care of it."

"Thanks, Tom. I appreciate it."

I ended the call and quickly pulled up the file I had been holding on to. I sent it to him and put the phone away. It was done. I had just hammered the final nail into the Savage family coffin. Three years of tirelessly working to take them down had come to an end. All I had to do was sit back and watch it happen. It was what I had wanted from the very moment I realized what Elly had done.

So why didn't I feel elated? I was fucking miserable.

It was her. And she had a hold on me that I couldn't break free of. I wasn't sure I would ever be free of her ghost. She would haunt me for the rest of my days. Would I ever find peace? Love? Real happiness like Wes and Rian had?

I was convinced it would never happen. Not for me. It was my curse. I had fallen for the wrong woman. I was doomed to spend the rest of my days wanting what I couldn't have.

CHAPTER 2

ELLY

I couldn't keep my lip from curling with disgust as I was jostled from one side to the other of the busy city sidewalk. There were so many people. None of them bothered to say excuse me or seemed to notice I was carrying a toddler on my hip with my other arm behind me dragging my suitcase. Every jostle threatened to throw off the very precarious balance I was managing.

It was a cool, dreary day, but I was sweating like a damn pig. The people and the extra weight of my two-year-old and the stupid jacket I'd thought I needed was too much. I could feel my anxiety ratcheting higher and higher with every bump.

I inhaled through my nose, praying for patience. Lizzy started to fuss. The long day of traveling had left both of us exhausted and cranky. I was hungry. Lizzy had been snacking off and on since we'd left sunny Los Angeles, but she needed an actual meal.

"Just a few more minutes, sweetie," I promised. "We're almost there. Then you can run and play."

"Hungry," she whined.

"I know. We'll eat some dinner as soon as we get to Grandpa's."

I looked up, checking the addresses on the buildings as we passed. I had been more than surprised when my dad gave me the address. I asked why I wasn't going to the apartment on Fifth Avenue, but he didn't give me an answer. The address was another in Manhattan, but not in the same vicinity of.

"This is it," I said, walking toward the door of the building. I released the suitcase, prepared to juggle the baby, open the door, and then grab my suitcase before it could be snatched.

Like an angel from heaven, a doorman opened the door for me, offering me a warm smile as he grabbed my suitcase for me. "You've got your hands full."

I laughed. "I do. Thank you so much."

"Are you visiting someone?" he asked.

"Actually, I'm going to be staying here. My father is Ron Savage. He said he would leave me a key."

The man smiled. "Ah, you must be Elly, and this little lady must be Lizzy. I have your key for you."

I followed him to his small desk. He pulled out the key and handed it over.

"Thank you so much."

"Can you get to the elevator okay?"

"Yes, thank you."

I got inside, my arm on the verge of giving out, but I was not about to release Lizzy. I didn't want to chase her, and I knew she would take off running the minute her little feet hit the floor. I waited for the elevator to stop moving before grabbing the handle of the suitcase and heading down the hall.

I found the right door, fumbled with the key, and managed to get the door open. "Dad!" I called out into the dark, chilly apartment that exuded a musty odor. "Dad, are you here?"

"Papa!" Lizzy called out.

I smiled and gave her a quick peck on the cheek. "I don't think Papa is home."

I flipped on the light and almost recoiled at the sight of a kitchen littered with dirty dishes and empty takeout containers. There were a few newspapers tossed on the floor next to the sofa and a few empty bottles of beer.

"That's new," I muttered, leaving the suitcase but keeping Lizzy on my hip.

I turned on another light as I walked farther into the apartment. It was big—not Fifth Avenue big, but it wasn't a hovel. I headed for the short hallway, opening one door and determining it must be my father's room before turning to the other door.

"This is it," I told my daughter, flipping on the bedroom light.

I scanned the room, empty except for the chest of drawers, a queen bed, and a nightstand. It was relatively toddler safe. "Okay, you can get down, but stay here," I ordered.

She wiggled in my arms until I put her on the floor. I walked back into the living room with Lizzy right on my heels. The first thing I did was pick up the empties scattered around the living room and toss them in the trash.

"What the hell?" I mumbled under my breath as I looked around at the trash.

My father had called me a week ago, frantic and demanding I drop everything to fly back to New York. He had freaked me out. I had taken a leave of absence from my job, packed up my kid, and hightailed it home. He knew when my flight was coming in and hadn't bothered to show up at the airport or even send a car.

"Let's go look in Grandpa's room," I said, trying to make my need to snoop sound like an innocent game.

Lizzy followed me down the hall once again, getting some exercise in her poor little legs that had been confined for almost six long hours. A shirt that I assumed belonged to my father was tossed on the bed. I opened the closet and saw a couple of shirts hanging, but otherwise, it was empty.

I walked to the dresser and pulled open drawers. A few leftover articles of clothing from what looked like a rush packing job. I frowned, putting my hands on my hips and looking around. Maybe he'd had an emergency business meeting out of town.

"Let's get our suitcase and we'll get your toys," I said to Lizzy, who was opening and closing the drawers.

After unpacking the suitcase and making use of the dresser and empty closet, I went back to the kitchen to see what I could put together for dinner. I had thought he would at least take us out. Clearly, he couldn't be bothered.

"Are you hungry?" I asked Lizzy.

"I want crackers," she answered.

I laughed. "Let's see if we can find something a little more nutritious."

I opened the fridge, took a glance, and quickly shut the door. The smell of sour milk nearly made me vomit. I had a feeling the cupboards would likely be bare as well. I had to tamp down my anger. I couldn't believe he had demanded I come home and then disappeared, leaving us with a filthy apartment and nothing to eat.

I grabbed my phone and hit the Redial button. I had called when we landed. I called when I couldn't find him at the airport. I called from the subway, and each time it was the same thing—voicemail. "Dad, it's me. We're at the apartment. Where are you?"

I searched my contact list and found his office number. I almost never called him on the line, preferring to use his cell. The call went to voicemail as well. I didn't want to leave a message on the company line and simply hung up.

I glanced around and shook my head. I had no idea where he was or what the hell was going on. If we were close, like we had been before everything happened, I probably would have known earlier that something was wrong. As it was, we talked very little. I had lost a lot of respect for him when he'd essentially forced me to go in and steal information. He'd used the information and cost me everything.

He didn't care what the fallout was. And as if being used and lied to wasn't bad enough, he screwed up a deal that I had helped put together. A deal that had destroyed my life and never made the company a dime. It should have. If my father wouldn't have screwed it up, he could have made millions. I had seen the projections. I had seen the potential earnings, but he made almost nothing off the deal.

When he'd called last week, he claimed the company was on the brink of ruin. He begged me to help. I had refused, but he made me feel guilty for leaving in the first place. I shouldn't have felt guilty, but he had a way of laying it on thick.

He used his one card—my mother. Whenever he wanted to guilt me into helping him, he brought up the fact that he was all alone in the world. When she died, there had been a huge hole in our lives. It was hard to imagine a single person taking up so much space in the world that when they died, there was a huge vacuum. Her absence had been almost impossible to cope with until I realized I had to be strong for him.

I had grown up almost overnight, taking care of him. It gave me something to focus on—a way to avoid my own pain. It wasn't until my world was turned upside down three years ago that I realized he'd been selfish. He'd used me over and over. I had been too naive to see it then, but my eyes were wide open now.

I didn't want to see him financially ruined. I didn't necessarily respect him, but I did love him in a distant way. I had come home to try and help him fix what he had broken, and the guy didn't even have the decency to be around.

"Nice welcome home, Dad," I muttered before flopping onto the couch.

Lizzy was playing with one of her favorite toys, content with the new surroundings. I watched her play. Her hair was growing darker by the day it seemed. She had started with my pale blonde hair, but it wasn't meant to stick around obviously. Her father's genes were stomping all over mine. Even my blue eyes that she'd been born with were gone. They were a pretty hazel color that I loved, just like his.

I pulled up my Uber Eats app and browsed through my choices. I picked Italian. Lizzy loved spaghetti. It was messy as hell, but she deserved to get a little messy after the long day she'd had. With dinner ordered, I dropped my phone on the couch and headed for the window to check out the view.

My eyes roamed over the city streets below and the tall buildings lining both sides of the street. A few years ago, I loved the view. I loved the city. Now I looked down and I saw chaos and darkness. Southern California was so much brighter, and not just literally. The sun had a way of making things look cleaner and fresher.

I reminded myself I wasn't there to stay. I still had my place back in California. I was only in New York for a little while, until I could figure out what the hell was going on. Then I was out. Lizzy and I could not stay in the city. We were doing just fine by ourselves in Los Angeles. I had been taking care of myself for so long, I didn't remember what it was like to have someone take care of me.

"Momma," Lizzy said, toddling toward me.

I smiled and turned to face her. "We should change you into something comfy," I said, scooping her up and carrying her back to the bedroom.

We had started potty training a couple of months ago, and by some miracle, it worked. I had put her in a pull-up for the flight, but she'd done very well. I was very proud of my baby girl. She was a very smart girl, just like her mommy. And daddy I supposed.

"All right, kiddo, let's go get our dinner," I told her when I heard the doorbell.

It wasn't exactly how I envisioned my first night in the city, but then again, it was probably for the best. I was tired and cranky after the long day of travel and didn't have it in me to deal with my father. Tomorrow I would be ready to tackle the mess he'd created.

CHAPTER 3

DEVIN

I exited the black town car, closing the door behind me and tapping the top of the car to let the driver know he could go. I buttoned the jacket of my suit and walked toward the door. A doorman opened it for me. I smiled and walked inside, pulling off my dark sunglasses and putting them in my inside pocket. Then I gave my name to the receptionist and was told to have a seat while I waited.

The start-up company was doing very well judging by the size and location of the offices. The interior was nice—not as nice as my own offices, but nice, nonetheless. I checked my watch. I was about ten minutes early for my meeting with the owner of the firm I was about to steal out from under Savage's nose. I had done my homework and was confident I had the offer that would seal the deal.

It would be the final blow to Savage's company. I almost wished I could see his face when he discovered it was me that had taken him down. I smiled, walking toward one of the chairs and about to sit down when I heard something that made my blood run cold.

I spun around, my eyes scanning the area. I had to be hearing things. "Fuck me," I hissed on an exhaled breath.

Ron Savage had just walked in, and beside him was his scheming daughter, Elly. I couldn't believe my eyes or my ears. She laughed at something her father said and I watched in horror. Then excitement. Then I felt the familiar desire. My blood was running hot and cold, leaving me feeling very out of sorts.

God, I had missed her. I had dreamed of her almost nightly. Seeing her in front of me—I wasn't entirely sure it was real. Ron said something, and she let out another soft laugh. Watching the two of them laugh quickly transitioned my happiness at seeing her into fury. They were thick as thieves. I imagined they were laughing at me. I stepped forward, my jaw set in a hard line. I didn't know why they were there, but I wanted to take the opportunity to let them both know I had won. I knew my deal was far better than anything they could offer. I was the better choice, and the CEO, Toby Michaels, knew it. The Savages, a name that was befitting of the father-daughter duo, didn't stand a chance.

"What are you doing here?" I snapped.

Elly's eyes practically popped out of her head as she looked up, seeing me for the first time. Shock crossed her features. Her father stepped in front of her, a shit-eating grin on his face as he looked me up and down. I wanted to knock the smile off his ugly mug.

"You're a little too late, McKay," he sneered. "This deal is mine. You may as well crawl back to your office and tell Daddy you fucked up again."

I heard a sharp intake of breath from behind me. I glanced back to see a man with remarkable green eyes wearing a tailored suit staring at Ron and me. The man looked like he was chewing glass. "Mr. Savage, Mr. McKay, thank you for coming," he stammered.

"This is a done deal," Ron said. "It's mine. Go home."

"Sir, we're still considering offers," the man said.

I looked at the man, wondering exactly who he was. "You are?" I snapped, pissed that what was supposed to be an easy close was quickly turning into a clusterfuck.

He extended his hand. "I'm Toby Michaels, CEO," he said, his eyes glancing over to Ron, who had stepped forward.

I shook Toby's hand and once again found my gaze being pulled toward Elly. She looked gorgeous. She was wearing a skirt suit, tailored to fit her slender body and showing off plenty of leg. Her high heels made her look much taller than she was. I remembered the feel of her petite body climbing over me, rubbing against me, writhing under me.

Her hair was shorter than it had been when we'd been together. It was cut in choppy waves that were lighter than I remembered. There were subtle differences in her, but other than a new haircut, she was the same Elly that had made me fall for her tricks and schemes. I had to remember that. I had to remember the pain, or I would fall right back into the deep blue oceans of her eyes and find myself adrift once again. Her eyes were purposely avoiding me. I wanted to grab her and yank her into a room and demand an explanation. I wanted to ask her to her face why. Why had she screwed me over and then left without so much as a 'fuck you'? Once I said the words, or maybe before I said the words, I wanted to push her body against the wall and ravish her.

My attention was pulled back to Ron's raised voice. I pushed aside all thoughts of ravishing Elly's perfect body and stepped closer to where Toby had retreated. "Sir, I have an appointment with Mr. McKay," I heard him say.

"Yes, Ron, run along," I snapped.

"Bullshit," Ron hissed. "This is my deal."

"Not anymore." I smiled. "I have a meeting with Mr. Michaels, and I'm certain he and I will come to an arrangement that benefits his company more than you ever could. You should just go home."

"I didn't say that," Toby quickly interjected. "We are entertaining *all* offers. I agreed to take the meeting to hear your proposal."

I smiled at him. "Trust me; once you've heard what I have to offer, you won't want to waste your time with Savage."

Toby looked from me to Ron, clearly uncomfortable. Ron looked like his ears were about to pop off his head. He was apoplectic. His face was red, and there was spittle collecting at the corners of his mouth. "McKay," he growled.

Elly stepped forward and put her hand on her father's shoulder. There was an immediate change in his demeanor. He smiled at me, folding his arms over his chest and taking a subtle step back. Once again, Elly was stepping up to do his dirty work. All thoughts of ravishing her vanished as I stared her down, her hard gaze meeting mine. I knew that look. It was pure determination.

"Hello, Mr. Michaels, I'm Elly Savage," she said with a thin smile. "I think you need to consider the fact we've been negotiating a deal in good faith. For you to abandon those negotiations and not equitably consider both offers would be a mistake."

"I—" Toby opened his mouth to say something, but Elly was in beast mode.

Her tone was firm and a little on the icy side, a contradiction to the smile on her face. "You see, if you decide to jump ship at this point in the negotiations, I'm afraid our only recourse would be to make it known that your word doesn't stand for much. No one will be investing in your company. Your potential IPO will be in jeopardy."

Toby's mouth fell open, fear filling his eyes. I almost smiled. She was good—too good. I couldn't help but be impressed by the woman. She was cutthroat. A trait I would normally admire, when we weren't on opposite sides of the fence.

"I think I have a solution," I offered.

Toby looked at me, silently begging me for help. It wasn't a great solution, at least not quite as easy as I would have liked, but it would give me the satisfaction of thoroughly kicking Savage's ass.

"You'll withdraw and go away?" Ron sneered.

"Not going to happen," I spat. "I propose a representative from each of our firms sit down with Toby here and go over the offers. We'll work together to come up with something that is best for Toby's company."

Ron was practically drooling at the idea of getting in a room with me. I could see it on his face. He actually rubbed his hands together. "Perfect."

"I think Elly should be the representative," I said with my own satisfied smile. "She has a much cooler head, and the negotiations won't be derailed by flared tempers."

Ron's face returned to tomato status and once again, I feared his ears would blow off his round head. Elly put a hand on his forearm. "I can do this," she told him in a quiet voice. Part of me was jumping for joy at the chance to spend some time with Elly, while the other, rational side of me was kicking my own ass. I had no business going into a room with the woman. She was dangerous—toxic even. I was a strong man, I told myself. I could keep from falling under her spell.

"Great, then it's settled. Toby, does that work for you?"

He cleared his throat. "Um, yes, I suppose. It's unconventional, but if it keeps me out of the papers, I will do it."

"Dad, go ahead and take the car back," Elly said, turning to face her father, her back to me.

I had to look. Her ass, perfectly round and high in the tight skirt, threatened to pull me under her spell. I fought it and turned away. She turned back to face Toby and I with a smile on her face. "Ready?" Toby asked.

"Yes," Elly and I answered at the same time.

I gestured for her to step in front of me as we followed Toby into the conference room. I had to check out her ass one more time. It was too good not to look at it. I glanced over my shoulder and saw Ron watching us. I grinned, letting him know exactly what I was doing. The anger on his face was satisfying.

I turned back around and followed them into the conference room. Toby closed the door, gesturing for us both to take a seat. At that moment, the flight-or-fight sense took hold. I looked at Elly and realized I had to be some kind of crazy to put myself in a room with her again. It was stupid and reckless and threatened to destroy everything I had worked for.

I took a deep breath, calming my inner thoughts. This was a chance for me to exorcise the demon that was my desire for her. It would be my chance to be near her on my own terms.

Maybe, just maybe, it was the resolution I needed to the

ordeal, and I would be able to move on with my life once the deal was done. Once I had finished off the Savages and ran them out of the investing business, I could finally move on with my life and never think about those pretty blue eyes again.

CHAPTER 4

ELLY

My guts felt watery. Devin McKay was the last person I thought I would see. I knew he was in the city, but it was a really big city. I did not believe for one second our run-in was a coincidence. The man was smart and calculating. I had a feeling he had something up his sleeve. I had to find out what before things got ugly.

My first thought was; did he know? Did he know my secret? Was that what had brought him to the meeting? My first instinct was to run back to the apartment to check on my little girl. I had used a nanny service for the emergency babysitter situation. The woman came highly recommended and I felt safe enough leaving Lizzy with her, but I was still anxious. He couldn't know, I told myself. My secret was safe.

I turned my focus on the situation at hand. I knew Devin's company had the means to buy an entire team of lawyers that would drag out a court battle for years. He would have the best lawyers in the country working for him. My dad's lawyers, if he even had any, would not be able to compete. Devin would win. I glanced over at him, trying not to look directly at him. Looking at him was like looking at an eclipse.

It was dangerous.

I couldn't look at him and not remember what it was like to have his hands on me. His mouth. I inwardly groaned, my breath catching in my throat as I remembered his tongue and mouth and what he'd done to my body.

Stop.

He was toying with me—with my father. I knew him well enough to know he was up to something. He sat directly across from me. I could feel his eyes on me. I remembered something someone had once told me about not looking a wolf directly in the eye because it was considered a challenge, a fight for dominance. Devin was attempting to stare at me because he wanted to assert his dominance.

I wasn't going to let that happen. I collected my strength and met his fierce gaze. Butterflies took flight in my stomach the moment our eyes met. I felt twitchy and overheated. His hard stare was meant to intimidate me, but I would not be intimidated by him or anyone else.

I stared back, raising my chin and silently letting him know I wasn't bothered by his fierceness. *God damn, he's fucking gorgeous.* He looked the same as he had three years ago but with a hard edge about him. It was dangerous and sexy at the same time. His suit, Armani, with the tapered legs and low waist, was stylish and showed off his long legs and trim body.

But I wasn't there to ogle him. I was there to kick his ass out of the negotiations and preserve my family's legacy and my father's livelihood. It didn't matter how handsome Devin was or how much I'd missed him. I was back in New

York for one reason only. I was not going to get distracted by him.

"Thank you both for agreeing to meet with me," Toby said, pulling my attention away from Devin.

"You're welcome," I answered before Devin could. *Score one for me.*

"I'm thrilled to have caught the attention of both your firms," he continued. "I am looking forward to finding a solution to this situation. I want to clarify, there have been no official offers, good faith or otherwise. I'm not trying to screw anyone over."

I smiled. "Maybe not, but the fact you entered into negotiations with my firm is enough to imply you were interested in a deal. We consider that good faith and would have never met with one of your competitors because we value honesty and loyalty."

Devin scoffed before leaning forward. I could practically feel his body heat emanating from him and washing over me from across the table. "I think we can find a solution that works for all parties involved," he said, his voice buttery smooth. "I don't think any of us wants to waste valuable resources and time."

Toby nodded. "No, definitely not what I want."

"Have you reviewed our offer?" Devin asked.

"No. I briefly spoke with someone from your firm who gave me a general ballpark, but I've not seen anything in writing."

Devin scowled. "I had it sent over this morning."

"I'll check," Toby answered, pulling out his phone.

Devin and I waited in tense silence while Toby slid his fingers over the screen of his phone. I knew the moment he saw the offer. The man's eyes nearly popped out of his head. His jaw dropped and he looked up at Devin with the same look a little kid looks at someone offering them a jar full of candy. My heart sank.

My father couldn't compete with Devin. Not anymore. The company was in bad shape and was barely hanging on. Devin had the means to offer Toby the world. All I had were empty threats. If he called my bluff, it would be over before it ever started.

"This is..." Toby said, stopping and shaking his head. "This is generous."

Devin smiled. "It is a generous offer because I believe in your company. I think with the right funding, the right marketing, and some fine-tuning, you are onto something big."

"Thank you. That really means a lot coming from you Mr. McKay."

I cocked my head to the side, watching Devin preen. He was definitely up to something.

"However," Devin started, and that's when I knew I had been reading him exactly right. "I really can't get caught up in a lengthy negotiation process with a lot of back and forth. My firm has a lot of irons in the fire and tying up resources to fight a fight we could walk away from is going to be the best choice as far as my board is concerned."

I couldn't help but smile. I knew he had an angle. I couldn't wait to hear what the rest of his little plan was. I watched as Toby's excitement faded. "Oh, I see," he murmured.

"I am not inclined to walk away from this deal. When I believe in something, I am fully committed." Devin's gaze slid over to me like he was checking to make sure I was hanging on every word. He offered a smile before turning his attention back to Toby. "I want to make this work. I am not going to let the Savages get this deal for pennies on the dollar. I don't walk away from anything. When I want something, I stick it out."

His words were directed at me. I knew that. He was speaking to me via his message to Toby. "We would never try and shortchange Toby," I interjected, seeing the look on Toby's face. We were losing ground in a hurry. Devin could be very convincing.

Devin made a noise. I shot him a glare before turning back to Toby. "We were in the process of negotiating. You say what you want, we say what we want, you ask, we offer, and so on."

"I don't want to get caught up in a war between the two of you," Toby said, clearly uncomfortable.

I flashed a grin at Devin. I was getting into Toby's head, making him second-guess Devin's offer without having to up ours. "A war doesn't have to be the answer to this little predicament," Devin said, his voice tight.

"It's the only solution I see, unless you're willing to walk away," I said.

Devin looked me directly in the eyes and saw a glint of mischief. I shrugged. "I guess we're done here, then," I said, putting my hands on the table and getting to my feet.

"Wait!" Toby blurted out.

I looked at Devin, arching one brow. The ball was in his court.

"I'm not walking away," he said with a smile playing on his lips. "I don't believe the Savage firm is going to walk away, and I think I can speak for all of us when I say none of us wants to fight. I have a different solution entirely."

"What?" Toby said, the old excitement back. "I'm willing to listen to anything at this point."

"Yes, please tell us," I said dryly. "We're all dying to know."

That hazel stare turned back to me and I was paralyzed. I couldn't look away.

"We make a joint investment."

"What?" I gasped. "Both companies?"

He nodded, not tearing his gaze from mine. "Both. Together. A team."

"How would that work?" Toby asked.

Devin finally looked away. I had to keep my shoulders from slumping forward. I felt like I had been held in his firm grasp, and when he looked away, it was like being released.

"My firm and the Savages would only have to put up half of our original offers. Half the cost and half the risk."

"Is that a thing?" Toby asked, looking from me to Devin.

"It can be," Devin said. I knew it was coming. I braced myself. His eyes turned to mine once again. "If Elly is willing to work with me?"

He was putting me on the spot. If I said no, I looked like the bitch. I looked like the one who was pushing us into a battle. Toby wouldn't want to work with me or my father. Devin had set it all up perfectly, but why? Why would he want to work with me? He hated me.

I cleared my throat when I realized they were both staring at me. "I don't have a problem with that," I managed to get out.

It was like sucking on a lemon and trying to speak at the same time. The words were bitter and tasted foul on my tongue. I watched his reaction. It was satisfaction. *What the hell is his game?*

"Great!" Toby exclaimed, clapping his hands together. "That sounds great! What comes next?"

I looked at Devin, waiting for the answer. "Miss Savage and I will work out the details and get back to you," he said to Toby before looking back at me. "Can we set something up for this week?"

"I'll check my schedule," I answered coolly.

"Sounds good," he said, making a show of checking his Rolex. "I've got to run. I have another meeting. I guess you can have your assistant call mine, assuming you still have the number."

I cleared my throat. "I'm sure someone does," I answered.

"Good," he said, getting to his feet. He towered over Toby and me. Toby got to his feet as well. I stayed in my seat, watching as they shook hands. "Miss Savage," he said before walking out.

I let out a breath, pulling myself together before getting to my feet as well. "It was nice to meet you, Toby."

"I'm sorry about the confusion."

I smiled. "I hope we can work this out," I said, not letting on that it had all been a very elaborate bluff.

"I'll walk you out," he said, being the perfect gentleman.

I walked out to the lobby, not thrilled to see my father had stuck around. Judging by the look on his face, he'd seen Devin leave. Those two were like oil and water. No, that wasn't accurate. It was more like fire and gasoline.

"Let's go," I said in a low voice when he came toward me. I didn't want to get into the details of the conversation with Toby nearby.

"What's going on?" he growled. "McKay just walked out of here like he'd wiped the floor with you. Don't tell me you rolled over for him."

I stopped walking and turned to face him, my finger up and close to his face. "Don't you dare. I'm here to do you a favor. Do not make me regret coming back here."

He backed down immediately. "Fine. What happened?"

I wasn't looking forward to telling him. I was still pissed about his little disappearing act and then calling late last night and telling me about the meeting. He'd given me almost no time to prepare. I had been up most of the night going over the documents he had emailed. It was a good deal and it could turn things around for him. He had refused to answer my questions about where he was or where he was staying, which was odd, but not my biggest concern.

I quickly gave him the abbreviated recap. He was oddly enthused about the idea. I had a feeling he thought the whole thing was going to be a replay of the last time Devin and I had worked together.

Not a chance in hell.

CHAPTER 5

DEVIN

I walked into my private bathroom, smiling in the mirror and turning my head left and right to make sure there wasn't anything in my teeth. Satisfied my teeth were clean, I straightened my tie; it was power blue. And sitting against the black of my tailored shirt, it stood out even more so. My jacket was black as well. I had taken to wearing a lot more black after Elly had fucked me over. I liked black. It made me feel dangerous and edgy. I had been left feeling like a putz after the whole debacle and probably deserved to wear pink.

Black gave me strength. It reminded me to never be soft again, to never openly trust again. I walked out of the bathroom and took my seat behind my solid cherrywood desk, befitting of a powerful man. I looked around my huge office, at the deep mahogany walls and the brown leather furniture. It was all very masculine.

I wondered if she would notice the changes. I had gotten rid of the stupid paperweight she'd given me. I replaced the picture of a beautiful beach sunset that had been hanging on the wall with a dark abstract. I had even replaced the light fixtures with the beige shades with dark red. Would she notice? It didn't matter, not really, but the changes were all part of the man I had become.

I was looking forward to seeing her again. I hadn't been able to think of much of anything besides her since I had seen her last. I couldn't wait to be alone with her. My plan to have us work together was pretty fucking genius. I wanted to make her squirm. I wanted to keep her guessing. I'd lead her on, play nice, and let her think I was serious about sharing the deal with her and her father.

Then I'd drop the hammer and yank it all away from her. I would let her feel the sting of betrayal, let her go back to her dear Daddy and admit she had failed. I wanted her to know the shame of being a failure. I wanted Ron to look at his precious little girl and see her as a disgrace. I wanted her to hang her head in shame.

As pissed as I was at the woman, I didn't necessarily want her to hurt. It was him I wanted to hurt. I wanted her to know she had not defeated me. I had risen up and grown stronger despite her attempt to take me out at the knees. I needed her to look at me and be worried. I wanted her to look at me and regret what she had done.

I wanted her to see me as a strong man. I needed her approval, and it pissed me off more than I cared to admit. I had been working my ass off for three years to prove I wasn't the chump she'd made me out to be. I hated that I needed her approval, but deep down, I did. "Sir, your ten o'clock is here," my assistant's voice cut through my musings.

I smiled. *Showtime.* "Show her in, please," I said.

I got to my feet, standing behind my desk as I waited for her. I didn't need to shake her hand. We didn't need to pretend when no one was around. The door opened and

Elly came through. She was wearing a fitted skirt that fell just above her knees and a white silk blouse with the top two buttons undone. It was casual and sexy as hell. Her hair was left in the same loose style she'd worn yesterday. It softened her look, giving her a youthful quality that contrasted the severe black and white of her outfit.

"Have a seat," I said, gesturing to the leather tub chair across from my desk.

She sat, purposefully crossing one leg over the other. I watched as she scanned the room, and I saw the moment she noticed every change. She gave a nearly imperceptible nod, which I doubted she even knew she was doing. It was something I had liked about her. She had a very expressive face. I knew when she was happy, turned on, angry. Of course, to her credit, I didn't know when she was lying directly to my face.

When her gaze finally met mine, it was one of defiance. She thought she had the right to be irritated with me for bothering her and making her climb out of whatever ivory tower she'd been holed up in. There was an air of arrogance as she looked down her nose at me. She was proud of what she had done and obviously thought I would be an easy mark a second time as well.

It didn't take me more than once to learn my lesson. Her deception and betrayal had been harsh enough to leave deep scars. She had taught me a great lesson that I would never forget. She wanted to play. This was a game, and she actually thought she had a chance at winning.

Not a chance in hell.

I certainly admired the confidence she was exuding. Looking at her now, I saw that same wide-eyed stare. Her face was that of an angel with the smattering of freckles across her nose and just a hint of eye makeup that made her blue eyes even bluer.

That stare was my kryptonite. It weakened me. It made me want to give up my plan and beg her to take me back, no matter what she had done to me. I wanted to pull her into my arms and kiss her senseless. I wanted to tell her how much I missed her and how bad I wanted her. I wanted her to apologize and tell me it was all a mistake. She'd beg for my forgiveness, and I would happily give it with the promise we would never lie to one another again.

No. She wasn't to be trusted.

"Well, I see nothing has changed," she said, folding her hands together and resting them in her lap. There was a smug look on her face, as if she thought her refusal to acknowledge the obvious changes would get to me.

I shrugged. "A little has changed."

She pursed her lips. "It's darker in here."

"That's not all," I shot back.

She made a face. "Your hair is a little longer."

I avoided the need to touch my hair. "Yours is shorter."

There was a thick tension between us. It was like two circling animals ready to fend one another off. Two tigers fighting over the same single raw, bloody steak. It was all about who could strike the fastest and hardest. I had been preparing for this moment for three years. I was essentially a fighter on the balls of my feet, my arms up and ready.

"What is your plan, Devin?" she said with heavy exasperation. "This isn't an accident. I know you well enough to know this was all orchestrated by you from the very beginning. What do you want?"

That was so typical of her—cut right to the heart of the matter. "Our firms have always been at odds. We've always competed against one another. I'd like to put all of that aside and form an alliance—on this one situation. Maybe it would be the start of something new. You have to admit there is a great deal of benefit for each of us to share the risks on an investment."

"And the rewards," she answered.

I shrugged. "Of course. That's why we do what we do, isn't it? We invest money in order to make money. Why not do that together?"

A thin smile spread over her lips. She leaned forward, her hands resting on the edge of my desk. "Why? Why would you want to work with my father when you've spent so much of your time trying to dismantle his company, brick by brick?"

I put on my most innocent face. "Because it's a beneficial union."

"Bullshit," she snapped.

I leaned forward as well, catching a very nice view of her cleavage. "I did hear your father's firm has hit a rough patch. That's unfortunate."

Her eyes narrowed. "Yes, unfortunate. Do you truly expect me to believe you just happened to stumble onto this same start-up? As I understand it, Toby hasn't yet figured out how to approach more than one firm to grow his company. Is it a setup?"

"You give me too much credit. Your father knew about the start-up," I reminded her.

"He did, through friends. Back to my original question, what do you want?"

"A partnership," I repeated with a fake smile.

She leaned back. She looked me up and down, her gaze scrutinizing me. "What do you get out of this partnership?"

"I told you, less risk."

"I don't believe you," she countered.

I shrugged, leaning back, laying my arms on the armrests. "Like I said, I heard your father is in a bit of a tight spot. I can help. This deal could be the foothold he needs to climb out of the hole he's made."

She slowly shook her head. "No. You're not doing this to help the man who snuck a deal out from under you. What is your endgame? What do you want from my father?"

My eyes drifted back down her chest, hoping for another little peek at her cleavage. If only I had some magical powers to flick open that one tiny, little button. I remembered the taste of her skin. If I closed my eyes, I could conjure up the image of her naked, her creamy globes with the perfect pink nipples jutting forward.

"I assure you I want nothing from Ron Savage," I murmured, trying to dispel the image of her naked body from my mind.

I heard her sharp breath and jerked my eyes up to see her glaring at me. "Oh my God," she breathed. "If it isn't him you want something from, you want something from me."

I smiled. "Tit for tat."

Her lip curled. "I should have known by the way you were looking at me."

I frowned. "How was I looking at you?"

Then it hit me. She thought I wanted sex. She thought I was going to demand sex in return for giving her dad a hand. The idea had never crossed my mind. Apparently, I wasn't all that great at the revenge game. I would have thought of that idea myself. It was good.

"I know you, Devin. I know that look in your eye."

She wasn't wrong. I had been thinking about sex. I probably did have that look she was referring to. "Elly, I don't know what you're talking about," I said, feigning innocence.

She shook her head. "I can't believe you. You know how important the company is to him, to my family."

I smiled and nodded. My mind was whirring. Was she actually considering the idea? My eyes drifted down her front and over the length of her legs. I would love another chance to be with her. I had craved her touch.

What could it hurt to take her up on her offer, whether she was actually offering or not? How far was she willing to go for her father? I had already seen what she would do once before—was she still willing to use her body to get what her father wanted?

I couldn't stop the smile from spreading over my face. It was the perfect revenge. I only wished I would have thought of it myself. Damn, Ron Savage was a ruthless man. I was going to enjoy destroying him.

CHAPTER 6

ELLY

I felt like I was on a roller coaster that I hadn't gotten the chance to check on before climbing in and being strapped down. I didn't know what was coming, but I knew the ride would be filled with lots of ups and downs and twists and turns. I was already feeling a little sick to my stomach. I had slept very little last night.

All night I lay in bed, wondering what the hell Devin was up to. What kind of revenge was he seeking? Something had to be motivating him to try and put together a deal that would require us working together. He certainly didn't need my father's money, influence, or power. In that respect, Devin held all the cards. He was the one driving the coaster, and I didn't like what that meant.

Last night or rather very early this morning, it hit me. He wanted me. Not wanted me in the sense a man wants to love a woman, but he wanted my body. He wanted to use me. Three years ago, when I had walked into his office for the first time, I had no idea what to expect.

From the very moment we had met, there had been

explosive chemistry between us. We both felt it. He flirted and I flirted back. He was so damn charming. Devin had been the older man that I was forbidden to touch. Of course, I'd touched. The forbidden fruit factor was no joke. I couldn't resist his charming personality and his good looks.

"Hello?" Devin's deep voice cut through my reverie.

I blinked, staring at the man who was staring right back at me with hungry eyes. Gone was the playfulness I remembered from our first time working together. Now there was a predatory look in his eye that was a little intimidating. And hot. *Goddammit!* Why was I still attracted to him?

"I'm sorry, you were saying?" I asked, keeping my voice cold.

"I think it was you who was making a suggestion," he said smoothly.

I frowned at him. It was like déjà vu all over again. I was right back in his crosshairs to try and save my father. Three years ago, my father had sent me to Devin's company to find out what Devin was up to. My father had told me Devin was a liar and a cheat and was working to steal a deal right out from under him. I had believed my father and wanted to defend him. I had risen to the challenge and played my part. I had never expected Devin to be the man he was.

And I had never expected to fall for the man that was my father's nemesis. But I had. I had fallen for him, and it turned my world upside down. Neither Devin nor my father knew just how much it had hurt me to learn the truth.

"I'm not making a suggestion," I managed to say. He was leering at me. His eyes locked on my breasts. I refused to squirm. I would not let him unnerve me.

"It certainly sounded like that to me," he practically cooed.

"What happened in the past is the past. It would be a mistake to do that again."

His smile grew and the lecherous look in his eye increased. "We have a very different idea of what qualifies as a mistake."

I shook my head. "Devin, what do you want? I am in no mood for games and I'm sure you have better things to do with your time."

That smile on his face only grew bigger. Had I only poked the proverbial bear? The way he was looking at me made my skin hot, and my insides were doing a dangerous dance of lust and desire. I couldn't want him. I couldn't be attracted to the man. He was dangerous. Being in the room with him was a risk I should have known not to take.

However, I had taken it for my father—again. I vowed it would be the last time.

"My time is my concern. We're here to talk about an arrangement that will benefit both parties. You've suggested I had ulterior motives. You put it out there, not me."

I cleared my throat. "I did, only to make sure you understand that one night was a mistake. Mistakes are meant to be learned from, not repeated."

Devin scoffed, his lips tugging up at the corners of his mouth. "That I completely agree with you on, but I'm not sure I would call what happened a mistake."

"I do," I said firmly.

He grinned, shrugging a shoulder. "We'll agree to disagree."

I fought the need to look down at my blouse to make sure all my buttons hadn't popped open. The way he was ogling me made me feel like I was stripped bare. How could one man's stare unnerve me so badly? I could practically feel his touch on my bare skin with the way his eyes continuously raked over me. It was making me crazy. I felt flushed and hoped like hell I wasn't blushing.

It was time to put an end to it all. I had the advantage. I had something he wanted. Something only I could give. I could leverage that to get my father what he needed to pull himself out of the giant hole he had created for himself. It was risky and completely unorthodox, but we were backed against a wall. I had to do something. I pushed aside all my apprehensions and general morals and turned on the sex appeal. I smiled at him and very slowly uncrossed my legs without completely flashing the man and then recrossed them. It got the reaction I was hoping for. I saw his nostrils flare as his eyes darkened. He stared at my legs, the skirt riding high on my thigh. I bounced my foot a little, watching his eyes focus on the red pumps I knew he loved. He had a thing for red. Like a bull.

"I think we could probably make a deal," I said in a husky tone.

He smiled and leaned forward. "I'm always eager to hear a proposal."

"Fine, I do have a proposal," I said. I offered him a coy smile, letting him draw his own conclusions.

His satisfied chuckle almost had me backing out of what I was about to do. He had planned on me offering myself up as the sacrificial lamb. He'd wanted me to do it. I hated that he felt like he was winning. Technically, I supposed he was. "I'm listening," he said, his eyes flashing with amusement.

"One night," I said, and my stomach churned. "I will be yours for one night. After our night, you walk away. You leave my father alone and you let him finish this deal he's been working on. You and I will never see each other again."

He leaned back, his hands pressed together as he pretended to consider the offer. He was going to take it. We both knew it was what he'd been angling for. It was all about the show. He wanted to drag it out. Maybe he expected me to beg. That wasn't going to happen. "One night?" he questioned.

"One night. That's it. Then you walk away from this deal. The terms of this agreement stay between us. No one, not my father, not Toby, no one knows how we reached the agreement. You can say whatever you want to preserve your image, but what happens will not ever, ever be discussed."

"Specific," he commented. "You've put a lot of thought into this."

"Not really," I said with a shrug. I could play it cool just as well as he could.

"This all just came to you?" He smirked. "I doubt that. You've thought about it, thought about your terms."

I knew he wanted me. I could see it all over his face. We'd worked closely together long enough for me to learn his body language. I wasn't the innocent young woman I had been back then. I was wiser and understood the power I had. I had felt his need, his desire. I saw that same desire when we'd bumped into each other in the lobby of the start-up. He still wanted me. It was my secret weapon.

"Specific prevents confusion," I quipped. "I don't want there to be any confusion about what this means."

He said nothing. I suddenly got the feeling he was about to laugh in my face. Maybe I didn't have the power I thought I did. Maybe I had just made a complete ass of myself. Was that his goal? Did he want to embarrass me? Humiliate me? I was already trying to think of a way to backpedal out of the situation. I could say I was joking; say I was testing him. Anything than admit I had actually offered him the use of my body in exchange for a business deal.

"Okay," he said and leaned forward with his hand extended.

I blinked. He was actually agreeing to it? "It's a deal?" I asked, my voice barely a squeak.

He grinned. "Be at my place tomorrow night."

"I—"

"Tammy, you can show Miss Savage out," Devin said, pushing the button on the intercom.

I looked at him feeling completely shell-shocked and wondering what the hell I had just done. "Shouldn't we discuss the details?" I asked.

The door opened behind me to the assistant I had met earlier. "Tammy will show you out."

My mouth dropped open. "When?" I asked, trying to make sense of it all.

"Tomorrow evening, let's say seven."

"This way, please," the assistant said, her voice firm.

I was being thrown out of the office. He obviously didn't trust me to show myself out. I tossed him a look over my shoulder. I was not going to show fear. "Tomorrow," I said.

"I look forward to it," he replied.

I felt a shiver run down my spine. Dread or excitement, I wasn't sure which. I walked out with my chin high, ignoring the looks I got from the other employees. Some would remember me. I refused to show any shame or guilt.

Tammy pushed the button for the elevator without saying a word. When the doors slid open, I stepped inside and turned to face her. Neither of us said a word as the doors closed. She didn't like me. I didn't care.

I wasn't sure if there were cameras in the elevator. I kept my composure, pretending I was just leaving a typical business meeting. The moment I was outside the building and a good block away, I stepped inside an alcove and leaned against the brick wall. I dragged in several deep breaths, trying to figure out what the hell I had just done.

I had just made a deal with the devil. The ramifications of my deal would likely haunt me for the rest of my days, but I couldn't back out. It was done. I pulled myself away from the wall, stepped onto the sidewalk, and proceeded to hail a cab to take me to the apartment.

I told myself I could spend one night with him and then walk away and never return. I would go back to my life in LA with my little girl. My dad could figure out his own mess next time. I was done. I was not going to keep putting myself in Devin's path to benefit my father. He was a grown man. If he kept digging himself into a hole, he was going to have to figure out how to fix it.

I was not going to sacrifice myself again.

CHAPTER 7

DEVIN

I tried to close my eyes and banish the images of her, but she wouldn't go away. I had tossed and turned all night. When I opened my eyes and saw it was too early to leave my bed, I tried to go back to sleep. I needed rest. She was haunting me. The dreams had lessened over the years, but after seeing her again, they had amplified again.

I had not been able to stop thinking about her since she'd walked out of my office. That wasn't true. I hadn't stopped thinking about her since we'd run into each other. I groaned. Again, not entirely accurate. She'd been on my mind since the moment I had laid eyes on her three years ago. She got under my skin, which I had always prided myself on being rather thick. I wasn't weak.

How was it possible that one tiny little woman, naive and wide-eyed, had taken me down? A one-night stand did not mean anything. At least it didn't use to. Then *she* happened. Sex with her one time had turned me into a man I didn't recognize. I was convinced she'd put a spell on me. I had been with plenty of women, and none of them had done to me what she had. She'd shattered me. I had never given a person that kind of power. Until her.

Tomorrow, she would be in my home. She would be offering up her body to me. She would be mine for the taking, but I wouldn't take her. I wouldn't fuck her. I would let her offer herself. I wanted her to feel raw and vulnerable, and then I would reject her explaining that mixing business and pleasure was a bad idea. She'd look at me, horrified and embarrassed, and I would feel a modicum of satisfaction. She would ask me why, and I would give her no reason. Nothing. It would be part one of my plan coming to fruition.

Part two would be me wiping Ron Savage off the map. He'd be bankrupt. His daughter would see him for the disgrace he was. The Savages would be nothing more than a distant, bad memory. She would realize her mistake in fucking with me. She didn't respect me now, but she would when I was through with them. Except the thought of having her again was making my mouth water. My cock ached with need only she could satisfy. Thinking about her was destroying my resolve to follow through with the plan. I couldn't falter. I was so close. The finish line was in sight. I just had to cross it.

"One little fantasy," I whispered. "One last time."

I closed my eyes, trying to conjure up a memory. I vividly remembered the first time I had ever laid eyes on Elly Savage. My assistant had brought her in, introducing her as my intern. She'd walked in wearing a shy smile and looking at me with innocence in her eyes. She looked like an angel dropped straight from the heavens. She'd worn no makeup; her long blonde hair had been pulled back in a ponytail, and her lips had a perfect pout. I initially thought she was too young to be an intern. Then I looked at her very womanly body and realized she wasn't.

I remembered when our eyes met, and that shy smile combined with a slight lift of one shoulder had done me in. My insides had warmed, and my dick had jerked to life. From the moment I saw her, I knew she was dangerous. I had avoided her for a week. I knew I couldn't be around her. She was a delicate flower, and I was afraid of the temptation she posed.

Everything changed when the manager of a project went on vacation. I'd been forced to pick up the project and needed help. Elly had been all too eager to offer. It had been a deal we'd been working on putting together for months. So I'd set aside my attraction to Elly in order to get the job done.

Elly was smart. She was observant and learned very quickly. She became an asset. I was impressed by her organization skills and her willingness to work hard, even when there was no real benefit to her. She wanted to help because she was eager.

I groaned, my conscious mind fading as I delved deeper into the memory. It was such a good memory. It was the memory I used when I needed relief from the ache in my balls. I was only a little ashamed to admit it had only been me and my hand and more bottles of lotion than I cared to admit since her. In true dream fashion, the images that played in front of me were a little hazy, lacking the vibrant colors of everyday living.

"Thank you for dinner," she said with that smile that turned me inside out.

"Thank you for staying late and helping me out with this."

She flashed another smile. "I can't believe no one else wanted to stay. This is a huge deal."

I sighed. "They don't get it. You do."

"I certainly do."

I dropped another stack of papers on the desk and tapped them with one finger. "I need one of these in each of the packets."

"Got it," she replied, grabbing the stack and sitting on the floor. She had been helping me put together the documents that I would be handing out in packets at the meeting that was being held at the end of the week.

I had been stressed about getting everything ready in time. There was so much riding on the proposal. It was going to be my first big deal. My first big move as the head of the company. I was grateful for her help. Without her, I probably would have floundered. She was a lifesaver.

"You don't have any other plans tonight?" I asked, sitting at my desk and stuffing more envelopes.

She softly laughed. "Nope. I'm a boring girl."

"You don't do the club thing?"

She groaned. "No. I have, but it wasn't my scene. I didn't like the bumping and grinding and the idea that everyone is there to get laid."

I chuckled. "You weren't?"

"No! I'm not like that!"

In the back of my mind, I thought that was impressive. She was a beautiful young woman. Instead of using her beauty to get ahead, she played it down. I got the impression she was hiding her true self. She was smart but didn't come off as a know-it-all. She was subtle, the type of person that was always listening. She didn't butt in, and she didn't push her opinions and ideas on anyone.

"You're going to go far in this business," I told her.

She giggled. "I'm not sure I'm cut out for all this. It seems very high pressure."

"Nah, it's not so bad. It can take a bit to get a deal put together, but the reward is awesome. There is nothing better than having your hard work pay off. This particular deal has taken months to pull together. It's going to be good—great."

She smiled and nodded but said nothing. I watched from my chair as she methodically stacked papers, making sure they were even before sliding them into a packet. She was meticulous, someone who couldn't be trained. It was just her way. I watched her work for several minutes until she turned and caught me looking at her.

"What's wrong?" she asked.

"Nothing," I answered, quickly pulling myself together.

I couldn't have the hot young intern. She was off-limits, I reminded myself.

"I need more folios," she said.

I nodded, trying not to look directly at her. "They are in the file cabinet."

She got to her feet and walked over to the tall cabinet and pulled on the top drawer. She yanked again. "Dammit," she muttered under her breath.

I chuckled and got up to help her. I had just moved behind her when she jerked hard again. The drawer gave way, sending her flying backward. I reached out to catch her before she could fall on her butt. My arm wrapped around her waist, automatically tugging her toward me.

Her body slammed against mine. She looked at me, her eyes wide as her gaze dropped to my lips. I watched as the tip of her tongue popped out of her mouth and licked her lips. It was the last straw for my willpower. I couldn't resist what I had been wanting for so long. Her soft, pliable body was in my arms, her mouth inches from my own.

One kiss, I had told myself. One quick kiss and that was all I needed to satisfy my longing for her. I gave her a chance to deny me. I looked into her eyes, almost hoping she would push me away. She didn't. Her eyes fluttered closed, and that was all I needed.

My lips touched hers, barely brushing over them before I went in deep. I turned her in my arms and pressed my lips against her, demanding her to open up and let me in. She promptly obliged, allowing me to sweep my tongue inside her mouth. I moaned into her mouth. I knew at that moment one taste wasn't going to be enough. I needed so much more.

My hands dropped to her hips, yanking her against me. I wanted her to feel how hard she made me. How much I wanted her. I heard her sharp intake of breath when she felt what she had done to me. She didn't pull away.

Her lack of pulling away was the permission I had been seeking. I deepened the kiss, holding her lower body against mine. The little vixen was grinding herself against me. She wasn't quite as innocent as she seemed. Her breasts rubbed against my chest, her hands reaching into my hair.

I told myself to stop. I told myself it was going too far. I couldn't stop. I needed her like I needed air. My hand reached around to unzip her skirt. I pulled the zipper down before wiggling the fabric over her hips. She lifted one foot, then the other, kicking the skirt out of the way.

I pulled my mouth away from hers and slowly unbuttoned her blouse before pushing it over her shoulders and down her arms. Her body arched, her breasts straining toward me. The red lace bra barely concealed her puckered nipples. My eyes traveled down her body; the matching thong was too much for me to resist.

I reached for her, yanking her slender body against mine. My mouth slammed over hers, taking what I had been craving for weeks. Her hands slid up my back while mine stroked down her sides until my hands were filled with her perfectly round ass. It wasn't long before she was tugging at my shirt, pulling it from where it was tucked into my pants. Her hands slipped under the fabric, splaying out over my chest as she massaged my pecs.

"Off," I growled.

I needed skin-to-skin contact. With my mouth still glued to hers, I undid the buttons of my shirt before stripping it off. She pulled her mouth away and planted it against my chest. Her hot, wet mouth suckled me. It felt like I was being branded. I hissed in a breath as her hands moved down my chest, unhooking my belt buckle and yanking open my pants.

My last coherent thought was something about not fucking the intern in my office and that thought was quickly pushed aside. Fucking the intern was exactly what I was going to do.

CHAPTER 8

ELLY

I wanted the bra off. I wanted my panties off. I wanted both of us naked. I had never wanted a man as much as I wanted him. The last few weeks working closely alongside him had been foreplay—a very long, drawn-out round of foreplay. It had left me aching with need.

I wrapped my hand over him through the cotton fabric. It was like rubbing a solid steel shaft. "I want you," I whispered next to his ear.

"You're going to have me," he said, his voice raspy. He pushed my panties down. While I kicked them and my heels off, he unhooked my bra. My breasts spilled out, caught in his hot hands. He massaged them before dropping his mouth to one nipple and then the other.

"Devin," I moaned. My body felt like I was on fire.

In one swoop, he lifted me, dropping me on the desk. I watched as he stripped off his pants, letting them fall to his ankles. I bit my lower lip, staring at the size of him bulging in his boxers. He was so much man. I wasn't used to men like him; real men. My eyes roamed over his chest, the smattering of black hair and the sexy trail over his navel that disappeared under his boxers.

I reached for the waistband of his underwear and frantically pushed them down. "Oh," I breathed, seeing just what it was he was packing.

His hand slid up my inner thigh, opening my legs. I didn't resist. I opened myself to him. His fingertips slid over my folds, opening me to him. I closed my eyes and dropped my head back, giving over to the need I had been fighting for so long. One thick finger pushed into my opening. I was already wet, easing the way.

"You're ready," he whispered.

I kissed his chest before sucking a swath of skin into my mouth. "I'm ready," I answered, looking up at him.

He didn't hesitate. He pulled his finger out before guiding his heavy cock to my opening. I whimpered as his thick girth pushed inside. It stretched me, sending brilliant sensations of pleasure and pain racing through my body. It didn't take long before my body adjusted and he was sliding inside me, inch by glorious inch.

"God damn, you're so fucking tight," he groaned.

"You're so big," I blurted out without thinking.

He released a combination of a groan and a laugh as he pushed himself impossibly deeper. My arms went around his neck, pulling my body closer to his. The close contact was all that was needed to send my body spiraling into a melody of fireworks.

"Oh shit," I gasped, waking myself up as my legs rubbed together, my pussy throbbing with the climax that had been the result of a very wet dream.

I looked over at the small bed that I had purchased for Lizzy. She was sound asleep. I rubbed a hand over my face before grabbing my phone off the nightstand and checking the time. It was just after seven in the morning.

I blew out a breath, trying to shake off the self-induced orgasm. I threw off the blankets and got out of bed, padding out to the kitchen to start some coffee. I hated that the man could still make me come without even being near me. The memory of our night together was often the thing that woke me up from an erotic dream.

I couldn't believe I was about to do it all over again. I hadn't recovered from the first time, and here I was preparing to march myself into the lion's den. I knew I should feel ashamed for whoring myself out to get something my father needed. But I couldn't feel ashamed. In my mind, Devin was my one. He hated me, which presented a bit of a problem, but I couldn't see it as anything other than two adults choosing to share their bodies with one another.

I knew he wanted me, and I damn well knew I wanted him. People my age had flings all the time. I preferred to think of my coming night with Devin as a thing, not an arrangement with sex being exchanged for a business deal

Truthfully, I needed sex—real sex. Not the sex that involved me and my vibrator back at home. I had gotten one taste of great sex and that was it. It was like getting one Dorito and never having another. I couldn't bring myself to sleep with another man. After I had done what I did to Devin and then found out I was pregnant, I'd fled, throwing myself into being a mother to our little girl.

I sipped my coffee and stared out at the view of the city. I felt very much like a caged animal. I was counting down the minutes until I had to present myself to him. *Had to* may not have been the most accurate way of saying it. I kind of wanted to.

I spaced out for I didn't know how long. It was Lizzy's

voice calling for me that pulled me out of the trip down memory lane. "In here, baby," I called out, walking down the hall to meet her.

She smiled, her dark blonde hair mussed as she walked toward me. I scooped her up and gave her a kiss on the cheek. "Are you hungry?"

"I want oatmeal," she answered.

I smiled. "Okay. You go potty and I'll make your oatmeal."

She toddled down the hall. I was glad she was awake. It would give me something to focus on. I had to keep my mind off Devin. My skin was super-sensitized; it always got like that after one of my dreams. Being back in New York and close to him had left me feeling very out of sorts. I had to remind myself he was a dangerous man hell-bent on revenge. I couldn't let my body's needs interfere with what my brain knew to be a risky situation.

He was a smooth operator and could very easily seduce me with very little effort. I had to stay focused on the goal. One night and then I was done. I would never see or hear from him again. It would be over. Devin and his gorgeous eyes and sexy body would be nothing more than a memory.

I spent the next several hours trying to stay busy. I played with Lizzy, cleaned up the apartment, and did an online grocery order. It was just after four when the doorman called. He asked if I was expecting company. I very happily told him yes.

I opened the door and waited in the hall. When I heard the elevator ding, I couldn't help but smile. It had been a long time since I had seen my best friend, Jane Middlemarch. She and I were very different, which could be why we got along so well.

Her bright red hair was piled on top of her head and she was wearing a pair of giant hoop earrings and a pair of skinny jeans and a tiny shirt that showed off her slender figure. "You bitch!" she shouted down the hall.

I burst into laughter. "I love you."

"I know, which is why you need to keep your ass here. You can't leave me alone in this city. You know I'm going to get in trouble."

I rolled my eyes, before throwing my arms around her. "You would get in trouble anywhere no matter who was around."

She giggled. "Let me see my best *little* friend," she said as we walked into the apartment.

Lizzy was sitting on the couch, a little bowl of goldfish crackers in her lap and her eyes glued to Mickey Mouse on the screen. "Lizzy, Auntie Jane is here," I said.

Lizzy barely looked away from the TV. "Hi," she mumbled.

"Clearly I left an impression," she quipped.

"Sorry. Mickey is very important to her."

"So, tell me, what brought you back to the Big Apple? I thought you said you were never coming back."

I groaned and jerked my head toward the kitchen. "I'm meeting Devin tonight," I whispered.

She raised her eyebrows. "Um, why? I thought we hated him."

"I don't hate him. He hates me. It's a very strange dynamic between us. It's like having a love affair with chocolate. So good, but so bad for you."

"Ah yes. But what do you mean meeting him? You asked if I could stay the night with Lizzy. That sounds a lot more like a hookup than a meeting."

"I agreed to stay the night with him," I confessed.

She put a hand on her hip. "You dragged your ass back to New York City for a one-night stand with your baby daddy? That is one hell of a booty call. What is that man packing that he can get you to fly across the country for a night of banging."

I scowled at her. "It isn't banging. And he didn't call me. He didn't even know I was coming. My dad got into some trouble. Turns out Devin is chasing the same deal my father is. The deal can make or break my father's company. My dad called me and asked me to help. That was before he knew Devin was involved."

"Are you sure he didn't know Devin was involved?"

I frowned and realized she was onto something. "I wouldn't be surprised."

"So, how is you staying the night with him going to help anything?"

"I doubt he's going to want to do a lot of small talk. We have nothing to talk about."

She raised an eyebrow and then very purposely looked at Lizzy. "No, nothing at all."

"He wants to take down my father. I offered to stay the night with him in exchange for him dropping his pursuit of the deal."

She laughed. "And he agreed to it?"

"Obviously."

"Wow. Is that smart?"

I shrugged. "I don't really have a choice. He isn't going to just walk away until he makes me pay in some way. Me submitting to him is what he wants. I know he's pissed about what happened. He needs to feel like he's getting back at me. This will hopefully satisfy him."

"Something tells me he won't be the only one satisfied," Jane teased.

I rolled my eyes. "I mean, he is fantastic in the sack that's for sure, and it has been a while since I've gotten any," I admitted.

"What if he asks where you've been or what you've been up to? What if you mention Lizzy?"

I laughed. "Like I said earlier, I don't think we're going to be doing a lot of talking, and I certainly don't think he gives a shit about what I've been up to."

"Elly, I know you still have some serious feelings for him. You are walking a very dangerous line."

She was right. "I have to," I said. "One night. I can handle one night. Once I know the deal is secured for my father, I'm out of here. I'm going back to California, and I'm not going to think twice about Devin or this city ever again."

She popped out her bottom lip before grabbing me and pulling me in for a big hug. "I'm sorry. I hate that you have to do this. I'll support you no matter what goes down. But I really don't want to see you hurt again. I know how hard it was for you the last time."

I hugged her back. "I'll be okay."

She released me and stared into my eyes. "I know you'll be okay, but I know it's going to be difficult."

"Thank you. I appreciate you taking time out of your busy schedule to watch Lizzy for me. I certainly don't trust my dad to do it."

She grinned. "Eh, it was just another party. You've been to one, you've been to them all."

"Still, I know you're a social butterfly. I do appreciate you doing this for me. The next time you come to visit, I will treat you to a spa day."

She grinned. "I'm going to hold you to it. Now, what are you going to wear?"

I looked down at the jeans and blouse I had on. "This?"

She wrinkled her nose. "I know this isn't a date, but you can't wear that. Aren't you supposed to be seducing him?"

I laughed. "I don't need to. I know exactly what he wants. I could show up in a paper bag and it would be fine."

CHAPTER 9

DEVIN

I was committed to saying no. I had been giving myself the longest pep talk of my life all day long. I could not fall into her trap. I could not let temptation rule. I had to reject her. I would let her play her part, let her work to seduce me, and I would pretend to be falling under her spell, but I would not succumb.

It was going to take every ounce of willpower I had, but my rejection of her throwing herself at me would be the ultimate revenge. She had used her body in the past, and I had fallen for it. Not this time. I was going to throw her words right back at her. I was going to tell her I didn't think it was a good idea to repeat past mistakes. She was a mistake.

I wanted to watch her face fall. I wanted her to be insulted and ashamed. I needed her to feel the same kind of blow to her pride that I had felt when I learned she had used me. It was a strange feeling, one that couldn't really be duplicated in any other way except by rejection. There was a specific rawness, a burning that was left behind after being used and tossed aside.

She had nothing that I wanted, and therefore I couldn't necessarily use her to get ahead, but I could certainly make her feel duped. I was counting on tonight to set me back on the right track. Ever since she'd used me and humiliated me, I'd been damaged goods. I could put on a good show, but inside, I didn't feel like a whole man.

I had been unable to trust another woman out of fear it would be a repeat of the Elly situation. I had a giant chip on my shoulder, and I wanted it gone. I wanted to be free of that ugliness. I was positive the only way that could happen was by taking back the pride and dignity she had stolen from me. I wanted to move on. I was desperate to close that chapter of my life. It had held me back for too long. I heard the doorbell. Normally, I would have the staff to answer the door, but they all had the night off. It was just me and Elly and my massive townhouse. "Showtime," I muttered to myself.

I opened the door, expecting to find her wearing something red, tight, and skimpy.

I was mistaken.

My eyes skimmed over the flowy light blue dress. Instead of the sultry siren I knew her to be, she looked like an angel. The latter was harder for me to resist than the first.

"I'm here," she said flatly, but I could see in her eyes she wasn't as put off as she made out to be.

I smiled and opened the door wider. "I can see that. Please, come in."

I reached for the collar of the light jacket she was wearing. She shrugged out of it, allowing me to hang it in the coat closet. "I've got dinner ready in the dining room."

"Dinner?" she asked with obvious surprise.

"Yes, I do eat. I'm assuming you don't only subsist on the blood of your victims."

She laughed, a light sound that echoed around the high ceilings and stark walls. "Cute."

I grinned. "I try. The dining room is to the left."

She walked through the elegant square entry that led into the formal dining room. The long table that could easily sit twelve dominated the space. The typical sideboard was against one wall with another serving station and my favorite, the wet bar.

"Wow," she said with genuine surprise. Obviously, she had been under the impression I would be clubbing her over the head and dragging her upstairs like a caveman. While the idea did have some merit, that was not the plan. I was going to put her at ease, be the perfect gentleman, and make her want me. By the time I wined and dined her, she would be putty in my hands.

Then I would toss her out. "Wine?" I asked.

"Please."

"Have a seat," I directed while I poured two glasses. I was doing my best to keep cool. Inside, I was dying to touch her. My cock throbbed. Being close to her was risky. I had to remind myself repeatedly that it wasn't going to happen. She was there only to serve as a means to an end. She and I were not going to fuck.

"It smells great," she commented as she took the offered glass of wine.

"I didn't cook it," I said, making it clear I didn't go to that much effort for her.

"I didn't think you did," she quipped.

I took my seat across from her. It was a little strange to sit down to dinner with my enemy. I did consider her my enemy. I had to. I lifted the silver dome from the main course before removing the lids from the side of buttered rolls and the salad.

"Please, help yourself," I told her.

She offered a small smile. "Thank you."

The tension in the room was thick. I knew we weren't going to have sex, but she didn't. She was going through the motions, trying to make something that was very abnormal, normal. I took a bite of the roast beef and waited. We both ate in silence for five minutes, only increasing the tension.

My eyes drank in the sight of her. Her hair was left loose and unstyled. It seemed to be a new thing with her. Before, she'd always had it styled in some way, either up or down, but she always looked like she had just stepped out of a salon. There was a change in her, like she wasn't quite as worried about her appearance. Like she had more important things to worry about than wearing designer clothes and keeping up with the latest trends.

She looked up and caught me staring. I didn't look away. It was part of the game. I wanted her to think I was sizing her up, preparing for a wild night together. It wasn't hard to look at her with lust in my eyes. I did want her. I wanted her more than I wanted the food on my plate or the wine in my glass. I would have loved to take her right on the table.

I was kicking myself for not putting on some music to drown out the silence. The dinner was not going as I had planned. I was supposed to be putting her at ease, getting her to let her guard down. That was the only way my revenge plan would work. She needed to believe I was going to have sex with her. That I would use her body and then never see her again.

"This is very good," she commented. "Your chef is amazing."

"I'll let him know," I replied. We fell back into the same uncomfortable silence. I had to do something and fast before she backed out. "So, what have you been doing with yourself these past three years?" I asked, trying to keep things casual.

She picked up her napkin and dabbed at her mouth. "I moved to LA. I've become a California girl."

I chuckled. It explained the lighter hair color and the even tan over her skin. "Really? What have you been doing there?"

She looked a little uncomfortable with the question. "I work for a venture capitalist."

"If you were going to stay in the investment field, why would you give up your position in your father's company and start over? LA is a long way from home."

Her eyes dropped to the food on her plate. She pushed the roast around with a fork, stalling for time. "I needed a change. It was time to see new places, meet new people, and just be me apart from my father's name and company."

"I see," I said, but I felt like she wasn't giving me the whole story. I wondered if there was trouble between her and her father. "I've often thought about doing that same thing. Just packing a bag and leaving it all."

"It isn't quite that easy, but I'm glad I did it. I like California. I like the weather, and I like the people. It's a very different vibe there. People are more laid-back, and it has been a good change for me. The air feels cleaner, and things are just, I don't know, better. Easier. More fulfilling."

"Did you completely start over, or is this venture capital firm run by someone you know?" I asked. I couldn't understand why she would give up her position in the Savage company. She would run the thing one day—would have. Ron had damn near destroyed it, and by the time I was finished with him, there would be nothing left to run, but she didn't know that. She had given up her family's empire to be a grunt in someone else's company. Something didn't feel right.

"No. All new. No ties to my dad or New York. It was a fresh start. I'm learning new things and gaining a lot of experience."

"I see," I said, not really seeing at all. It didn't make sense to me.

She was hiding something. Maybe it was her own guilt. She'd fled New York because she knew what she had done had been wrong. I wanted to believe that was the case, but deep down, I doubted it. She had known exactly what she was doing when she walked into my office that very first day under the guise of being an intern. Her seduction from that point on had been calculated and purposeful; there was no other reasoning behind it.

"What about you?" she asked.

"What about me?"

She shrugged. "You're in the same office, but has anything changed?"

I smiled, unable to keep myself from bragging a little. "The company is more profitable than it has ever been. We are doing very well under my leadership."

"Congratulations."

"Thank you. It's been a lot of work, but I like staying busy."

"I can definitely understand that sentiment."

I dropped my fork on my plate. I had made myself eat despite my lack of appetite—appetite for food, that was. I had a voracious appetite for something else, but that was not on the menu. "If you like LA and are thriving, why are you back in New York?" I asked.

My question made her uneasy. She squirmed a little, clearly not comfortable with truthfully answering the question. "My dad needed me," she said, her voice so low I almost didn't hear her.

"You gave up everything you've been working for over there to come back here and help out your dad?"

"It's a temporary situation," she said, her eyes meeting mine. That same defiance I had seen in my office was back

I couldn't help but grin. "Ah, I see. He needed you to deal with me."

"It isn't like that at all," she snapped.

I saw the flash of red in her cheeks and couldn't help but smile. I had hit a nerve. Good. It was only the beginning. I planned on hitting a lot more nerves as the evening continued. I wanted her raw.

CHAPTER 10

ELLY

What the hell was I doing? The whole thing was ridiculous. We were sitting down to a nice dinner like we were friends, lovers getting together to share a meal. We weren't friends. I had to constantly remind myself that he hadn't invited me over for dinner because he liked me. He hated me. He was trying to get closer to find my weakness.

I had fucked him over, and he wanted revenge. And that was even without knowing I was keeping his child a secret from him. Simply using my body wasn't going to be enough for him. He wanted to hurt me. He was going to try and get inside my head and then launch an attack. I knew it. I could feel it coming. Every sense was heightened.

I had to choose my words carefully. I couldn't accidentally say why or give any hints about what had really driven me to flee the East Coast. I felt like I was being interrogated. I wasn't sure how much he already knew about my life. I was relatively sure he had to have looked me up a time or two, especially in the weeks and months after what I had done to him came to light.

I would have if the roles were reversed. I would have stalked him and haunted him until I was satisfied I had gotten some kind of revenge.

"Your father has no problem making you his sacrificial lamb," he commented.

"Excuse me?" I asked.

"You just said you had made a nice little life for yourself in California, but you left it all behind to help out your father—again. You are putting yourself in my path because your father can't deal with me himself."

I wasn't going to let him goad me into saying something I didn't want him to know. "My father wasn't aware you were involved in this current situation when he called on me."

He smirked. "But he doesn't mind you seducing me again? I suppose if it gets him what he wants, he wouldn't care."

"I'm not seducing you."

"Aren't you?" he asked. "What does your father think about the deal you made with me to get him what he desperately needs?"

I looked away. "It doesn't matter."

His deep laughter made me want to throw a roll at him. "He doesn't know! You didn't tell him you were offering your body to me in order to get him the deal."

"It's none of his business. It's nobody's business. I told you part of the deal was no one could know. Do you really want everyone to know what kind of man you are?"

He raised an eyebrow. "What kind of man I am? Don't you mean what kind of woman you are?"

"This is between us," I hissed. "No one needs to know."

He scowled at me. "How exactly do you plan on explaining why I walked away from the deal? I won't have you making a fool out of me again."

"Don't worry about it. I will make sure your reputation is intact."

He scoffed. "I doubt that."

"You worry about holding up your end of the deal. I'm here. I'll do what needs to be done. That is my end. Once this is over, it's done. For good."

He glared at me, his hazel eyes flashing with anger. He jumped to his feet, throwing his napkin on the table as he glowered down at me. "There is no deal. You might be willing to trade on your body for a business deal, but I'm not. I will not touch you. My deal will move forward. I will close on it, and your father will be ruined, your family's legacy tarnished forever. Ron Savage will be the man that ran a multimillion-dollar corporation that he inherited from his own hardworking father into the ground. And you, you will be right there alongside him."

It was my turn to be pissed. I jumped out of my chair, and instead of throwing my napkin on the table, I threw it at him. It was a silly attempt to inflict harm. "You're toying with me!"

His slow, satisfied smile made me want to vomit. "I am."

"Why?" I shouted.

"You toyed with me, remember? Remember when you came into my office pretending to be a wide-eyed intern looking for experience? Don't tell me you forgot about your little time playing spy."

I was sick to my stomach. Furious with him and myself. I should have known it was a game to him. "You're a despicable man."

"That's rich coming from you," he spat.

"Whatever. This is over."

I turned on my heel and headed out of the dining room. I had to get away from him. I couldn't stand to look at him. My heels clicked against the marble tile as I made a beeline for the door. I would get a cab once I was down the block. My first and only thought was to get as far from Devin as possible. To think he'd gotten me over to his house just to point his finger and laugh at me was infuriating.

I reached for the door when I heard his footsteps behind me. "Elly," he called.

I refused to look at him. "What?"

"Don't forget your coat," he said, laughter in his voice.

I spun around, my eyes shooting fire at him. At least I wished they would shoot fire. Instead, I had to settle for a good solid glare. He walked toward me, that shit-eating grin on his face. I folded my arms over my chest and tapped my foot. He was taking his sweet time. I watched as he opened the closet and pulled it out.

He turned to look at me, my coat in his hand. I reached for it, but he snatched it back. "This is over. I will not be played with any longer. You and your father need to leave me the fuck alone."

"Whatever," I growled, reaching for my coat again.

He held it back. "I'm serious. I don't want any of your dirty tricks. Quit trying to seduce me. Stop making promises to sleep with me to get what you want. I'm done with all of it—you, your father, and his company."

I stared at him. There was so much anger boiling in my veins I worried I would erupt like a volcano sitting dormant for a thousand years. "You're done? No, asshole! I'm done. I wouldn't touch you if it meant I could secure a thousand start-ups. You can go straight to hell!"

I reached for my coat. My legs and hands were shaking with the fury flowing through me. He couldn't yank it back fast enough. I snatched it and jerked hard on the fabric. He released it at the exact wrong time. I went flying backward, my heels and shaking legs putting me off balance. My arms flailed as I tried to catch myself from falling on my ass.

It was his strong arms around me that kept me from hitting the hard floor. He pulled me forward, propelling my body against his chest. Time stood still for one very long second. Both of us, snarling beasts a moment earlier, stared into one another's eyes. It was a flashback to the first and last time we had kissed.

Neither of us made a move. His arms were around me, tight as a vice. My coat was in one hand, and my other hand was suspended in the air.

Then he kissed me ferociously. His mouth covered mine, hungrily devouring my lips with his. I opened my mouth, my own desire making me ravenous. The hand that had been suspended in the air moved into his hair. My fingers intertwined with the dark strands, none too gently. I dropped the coat and used my other hand to go to the small of his back and pull him closer to me. I was a hot mess of contradicting emotions.

I pulled him away by his hair and pulled him closer with my other hand. He seemed to be having the same problem. One of his hands rested on my ass, holding my hips in place as his body melded with mine. His other hand had tangled in my hair, gently pulling my head back and angling my face toward his.

The passion that had been on a back burner for years exploded into life. There was no stopping it, what was happening between us was visceral and completely uncontrollable. I began to tug at his suit jacket. I needed it off. I wanted to feel his skin against mine. In a flurry of jerking movements from both of us, we stripped each other down to nothing.

My heart was pounding so damn hard in my chest I felt like I was on the edge of some kind of medical emergency. I didn't care. My immediate concern was the throbbing in my pussy that was demanding attention.

He stopped moving, both of us panting as our arms hung at our sides. We were both naked, minus the socks he was still wearing. I barely remembered my clothes coming off. I stared at his body. It was just as I remembered. The broad chest, the hair over his pecs and navel, and the perfect V of his waist. My eyes moved lower. I sucked in a breath, staring at the jutting cock in the dim light of the foyer.

When I looked back at him, his eyes were filled with hunger. There was no stopping either of us. He lunged for me, pulling my naked body against his as his mouth slammed into mine once again. I turned feral, clawing at him, trying to climb his body.

His arms slid under my ass, lifting me up like I weighed nothing. One hand slid up my back, the other squeezing my ass. I wiggled, trying to find the right spot. I needed no readying. My pussy was slick with need for him. He slid his hand between us, guiding the tip of his swollen cock to my opening. Once I had my target, I was ready to move. I slid down his body and froze. There was a pinch of pain, my body not used to such encounters in the past few years. I pushed through the discomfort, letting his thick cock stretch me as he worked his way inside my body.

It only took a few seconds for my body to eagerly respond to the intimate invasion. I groaned with satisfaction. My body opened to him like a flower bud opening to the sunshine. I felt the tension leave his body as his arms wrapped around me, pulling me lower onto him. For one brief, beautiful moment, we stayed as we were.

Our bodies throbbed inside and around one another as our hearts banged against our chests. Once the moment passed, it became all about need. Lust pulled me out of that sweet moment and had me raking my nails down his back as I bounced on his cock. He grunted with frustration, neither of us getting what we needed to reach fulfillment.

"Fuck this," he growled, pulling out and dropping me to my feet.

I reached for him, desperate to have him inside me again. He hooked one leg around mine and took me to the floor in a soft tumble with his arm over my back to keep me from smashing against the hard marble. Before I had time to think, he was over me, driving himself into me. One thrust and I was sliding across the smooth floor.

He growled again, going to his knees and yanking me up to his thighs. He held my legs behind my knees as he thrust hard. I gasped, the power of his body taking me by surprise.

"Yes!" I shouted.

He thrust again before dropping me back to the floor and coming over me. His chest pressed against me as his mouth covered mine. He began to glide in and out of my body, taking me on a ride that teased and excited every nerve ending.

I was hopelessly lost as he did things to my body that made all the erotic dreams seem like child's play. I held on to him, digging my nails into his back and matching his thrusts with my open upward motion. In a flash, like being hit by a violent bolt of lightning, my body burst into a million rays of light.

I cried out, stiffening under him as I held on to him for dear life. I orgasmed so hard I felt like I was on the verge of passing out.

CHAPTER 11

DEVIN

Her lithe body turned to hot liquid around me. I felt her orgasm and had to pull my mouth away from hers to watch her face as I rocked her fucking world. Her eyes were squeezed shut, her lips red and puffy from my kisses. Her cheeks had red splotches of color on them, and she looked like the most satisfied woman in the world. Her nails scored my back as her own arched, sucking me deeper inside her tight sheath. Her pussy clamped down on my dick, massaging me as her orgasm rolled through her.

I kept moving, pushing my cock in and out of her, holding her in place as best as I could. Our bodies, slick with perspiration, slid across the floor. I couldn't get deep enough. I got to my knees and pounded inside her, watching her jerk, her mouth open as every thrust triggered another spasm. Her eyes popped open, her hand reaching to touch my face. I nibbled at her fingers until she pulled them away from my mouth and gripped my shoulder.

"That's it," I breathed. "Fuck you feel so good."

She moaned, her head moving back and forth. Her hair haloed around her as her perfect breasts bounced with every thrust. "Oh God," she groaned.

"I want another one," I demanded, determined to make her come again.

"I can't," she whimpered.

"Yes. You. Can." I thrust deep, rotating my hips and scraping myself against her soft heat.

She cried out, her hands gripping my biceps. Her nails dug in. I shouted at the pain that triggered a deep sense of pleasure I had never experienced before. Her body rocked up, nearly bucking me off. I bounced back, pounding my body into hers. Her whimpers and gasps of pleasure were pushing me close. I didn't want to blow my loud—not yet. I wanted to fuck her for hours and hours. I wanted to stay buried inside her until I had nothing more to give.

I was barely holding on. I was going to explode. Years of lusting after the woman had culminated in that very moment in time. My hand did not come close to the kind of pleasure her body could give me. It was the kind of pleasure that could never be duplicated. Only her body could make me feel this way. I braced myself, knowing it was going to be an all-consuming climax that made me feel like my head was going to pop off.

I roared as my body violently spasmed, erupting inside her hot passage. My head went back, my eyes squeezed tightly closed. I saw stars as my body spasmed and jerked inside her. I had no control over my thrusting hips. I damn near cried it was so good. I collapsed on top of her. I was instantly addicted. She had been everything missing from my life. My dick cradled inside her sweet pussy was what I had needed to feel alive again. I needed more of what we'd just done. I would never get enough. I knew that deep down in my soul. The idea that one more time would satisfy me had been a foolish notion.

I rolled off her, throwing one arm out to my side. The cool marble felt good against my heated skin. I dropped my other arm across my chest and stared up at the ceiling. The need for revenge had evaporated the moment her lips touched mine. I didn't need to hurt her or shame her.

I just *needed* her.

I could forgive everything that happened in the past. None of it mattered. I'd recovered. I was doing well. It was time to move on. I knew she felt something for me. There was no way sex between us could be that explosive without some kind of cosmic connection. There was an invisible pull between us.

I smiled and turned to face her. I wanted to see where she stood on our reunion. We had some kinks to work out, but I was confident we could overcome the little things we still needed to work through. I expected her to look at me with satisfaction and maybe a little bit of admiration. I had rocked her world. We both knew it.

Instead of a smile, she sat up, jumping to her feet and walking back to where it had all started. She started to dress, jerking on her panties and struggling with her bra. I got up and walked over to help her. "Where's the fire?" I asked in a husky voice.

She shrank away from me when my fingertips brushed over her shoulder. "Don't," she whispered.

"Elly," I said, questioning what was happening. Fear replaced the heat in my veins, sending a cold shiver down my spine.

My nakedness was suddenly a weakness. I reached for

my boxers and pulled them on, sensing the tenderness I had felt for her was all one-sided.

"I'll expect your official withdrawal by tomorrow morning," she said, her tone ice-cold.

"Excuse me?" I whispered, disbelief washing over me.

"You heard me. You got what you wanted. Walk away."

I turned my back to her, pulling on my shirt. I couldn't look at her. I couldn't let her see she had shattered me once again. Bile rose in my throat. My heart felt like it had been ripped from my chest and stomped onto the marble floor I had just taken her on. My ears burned with anger and embarrassment. I was a schmuck. How many times was I going to let the woman fuck with me?

"Walk away from a deal that could make my company a great deal of money?" I asked, trying to sound nonchalant.

"Yes."

I turned to look at her. Her blue eyes were turbulent. "This was a business transaction. I offered it up and you agreed to it. I kept up my end of the bargain, and now it is your turn."

I mulled it over. She was right. "I'll walk away," I quietly said. "I'll walk away, and you and your father better never darken my door again."

"Let it go, Devin."

"I will absolutely let it go, but here's the thing: it won't matter that I walk away. Your dad can go ahead and get the deal. The fact is, he's going to screw it up. He couldn't manage his way out of a paper sack. He's a fucking idiot and has no business sense. He's on his last legs and he knows it. It's sinking faster than the *Titanic*, and any smart person would avoid him and his black touch like the plague. He's going to take Toby down with him. It's going to destroy your father's reputation."

"Shut up!" she shouted.

"Truth hurts, doesn't it?" I sneered.

"You don't know what you're talking about. I've seen the deal. This is going to work."

I scoffed. "It could be a gold mine with a guarantee, and he'll fuck it up. Do you plan on screwing your way through New York City to try and save Daddy?"

Her mouth dropped open. She flinched as if I had physically slapped her. I knew the hurt she felt. She'd been dealing me the same blows since she'd walked into my life. I felt the tiniest bit guilty, but I refused to take back what I had said. I had to make it hurt this time. I had to make sure I would never let myself fall into her trap again.

"Fuck you," she hissed, bending over to grab her coat.

I didn't try to stop her. She yanked it on and was out the door before I could have tried anyway. I closed the door, turning to lean against it and gently bouncing my head against the solid wood. I closed my eyes, trying to pull my shit together. I was all over the place.

I had been the highest of the highs and then been dropped on my ass and was feeling the lowest of lows. The sharp descent had left me shaken to my very core. I had been on the verge of telling her I wanted her to stay. She would have laughed in my face, further destroying the modicum of dignity I was clinging to.

Once again, I acknowledged that only she had that kind of power over me. The power I kept giving her. I made a fist and hit the door. "Dammit! How fucking stupid can you be?"

I turned around and locked the door before walking into the study where I had the good stuff. I poured myself two fingers of strong whiskey and took a tentative sip. It burned as it trickled down my throat. It was exactly the feeling I had been going for. I took another, bigger drink and felt it burn deep into my belly.

I refilled the glass and headed upstairs. I wanted to shower. I needed to wash her off my skin. Even as I walked, I could smell her on me. I stripped off the clothes I had just put on and walked directly to my shower. I turned on the water, turning it down to a lukewarm spray. I stepped inside and let it wash over me.

I couldn't believe I had fallen for her tricks again. Well, technically, she hadn't tricked me. She came to my house with the intention of having sex. I had known that, but in my mind, I'd had no intention of actually fucking her. When it happened, it shook me to my core. I had foolishly thought it meant something different.

She had been about ready to walk out the door. The deal had been broken. The sex that followed had not been part of the deal in my mind. I had been wrong. I needed to accept the idea she felt nothing for me. Great sex did not mean feelings. She'd used me. Again. I kept falling under her spell. Every time I looked into those innocent blue eyes, I turned into an idiot.

"No more, Devin, no fucking more," I hissed, pounding my hand against the tile wall.

I stepped out of the shower, finished off the glass of whiskey, and crawled into bed naked. I didn't want to think. I just wanted sweet oblivion. Tomorrow I would rethink my plan. I said I would walk away from the deal, but what if I didn't?

"Be the better man," I said aloud.

I wasn't Ron Savage. I would never lower myself to his level. I didn't need Toby's company. There were a thousand more out there, just waiting to be discovered. I would find one. Hell, I'd find ten. Ron didn't know the first thing about properly vetting a company before he dumped his money into it, which was why he was in dire straits.

I always did my due diligence. Success was the best revenge.

CHAPTER 12

ELLY

I got out of the cab and rushed inside my apartment building. I couldn't bring myself to make eye contact with the doorman and just gave him a slight wave. I felt a little bad for being rude, but a conversation was just not going to happen. I felt so much shame. I couldn't believe what I had done. I was humiliated and disgusted with myself. I wanted to run away. I wanted to go back to California and forget all about my trip to New York. I hated my father for making me come back.

I slid my key in the lock and quietly opened the door. I saw the flashing of the TV and hoped like hell Jane was asleep. I couldn't face her either. She would want to know what happened. I shut the door, throwing the lock before kicking off my heels to keep from making any noise.

"Elly?" I heard her say.

I sighed. I wasn't going to get away without facing her. "It's me," I whispered. "Is Lizzy asleep?"

"Yes. She's in the room."

I walked into the living room and saw her with a blanket

on the couch. "I thought you would be asleep," I murmured. "I'm sorry if I woke you."

"I'm a night owl. You didn't wake me. I wasn't expecting you back tonight."

"Neither was I."

"Did you change your mind?" she asked.

"No," I muttered. "I wish. I should have. I should have never gone there in the first place. It was stupid."

She shrugged. "It was definitely a wild idea. I'm glad you walked away. What are you going to do about the deal now?"

I grimaced and rubbed a hand over my face. "I didn't exactly walk away," I admitted. "That would have been the smart thing to do. I'm obviously not smart."

"You are smart. You're the smartest person I know."

"Book smart maybe, but I'm clearly lacking in the common-sense department."

She laughed. "I don't know if that's true. I'll agree you aren't as world wise as I am, but that doesn't mean you're clueless. You tend to believe the best of people. I tend to be a little more jaded."

"You're not jaded, you're smart. I should have partied with you more."

"You were too busy studying, and that is a good thing."

I blew out a breath. "Do you ever feel like you're just making one wrong move after another? Like everything you do is wrong?"

She shrugged. "I probably do a lot wrong, but I just don't dwell on it. I like to keep moving forward."

"I wish I was like you," I groaned.

"I think you are perfectly you."

I wanted to smile. I couldn't. I was miserable. "I don't think I like myself very much. I'm not a good person."

"Yes, you are."

I slowly shook my head. "I'm not," I whispered. "No good person would do what I did."

"What happened?" she asked gently.

The shame I felt was a physical weight on my shoulders. I walked to the couch and sat down. Jane turned the TV down and looked at me, waiting for me to tell her.

"I hate him," I breathed.

"What happened?" she asked again.

"I got there, and he had a nice dinner waiting. We ate and tried to make small talk, but it was useless. Then, when I told him I was ready to do what had to be done, he told me it was a joke. He never intended to have sex with me. He only wanted me to offer myself to him so he could reject me."

She rolled her eyes. "What an asshole."

"Yes, he is, but that's not the worst of it. I ended up having sex with him anyway."

She frowned. "I'm not sure what that means. Did he force you?"

"No! God no. He'd never do anything like that."

"Okay, then he changed his mind? You guys brokered your deal?"

I nodded. "Yes, I guess you can say that. I was leaving and then I stumbled, and he caught me and the next thing I know, we were naked on the floor in the foyer."

"Wow that sounds pretty hot and heavy."

"It was, and I feel like shit."

"Why?"

"Because I pretty much used sex to gain money."

She sighed and shook her head. "You are not a whore. And if you're being honest with yourself, the sex wasn't just about business."

I couldn't hold back anymore. Tears sprang to my eyes, and instead of fighting it, I let them out. I bawled out the shame. Jane got up from the couch and leaned down, hugging me and rubbing my back as I let it all out.

I sobbed a little while longer before I decided I had cried enough. "I'm good," I said, rubbing my fingers over my face and wiping away the tears.

Jane got up and went into the kitchen. She returned a few seconds later with some paper towels. "I'm sorry, but you need to stay away from him. You can't let him control how you feel about yourself. You're a great mother. You are a loyal daughter, and you are my best friend. I love you. I know you are kind and generous, and your only downfall is caring too much."

I sniffled. "That's for sure. I have no reason to cry. I went over there to have sex with him, and that's what happened. I can't really be mad at him for taking me up on that offer."

"You can feel however you want."

I shook my head, shaking away the sniffles and the sadness I felt. "It's done. I got what I wanted. My dad has his deal, and I don't have to come back."

"I'm sorry you're going through this."

"Thanks. I'm good. Thank you for coming tonight."

"You're welcome. Don't leave town without saying goodbye."

I hugged her. "I won't."

I walked her to the door, locking it behind her before heading for bed. I knew I should shower, but I didn't have the strength. I was completely drained. I was so glad my dad wasn't there. I couldn't have looked him in the eye. As much shame as I felt, I felt just as much anger at him. He'd gotten us into the situation.

I didn't understand why he was doing what he was doing. He was on the verge of bankruptcy, losing everything. It was hard for me to understand how he had fallen so far. I had grown up wealthy. My grandfather had inherited a small amount of money and had turned it into a fortune. My father had inherited the company, and I thought things were going well. I had no idea he'd burned through the inheritance and practically ruined the company.

I closed my eyes, trying to pretend the last couple of hours had never happened. I was in bed alone. It was definitely not the way I had envisioned my night going. I'd thought I would be spending it in bed with Devin. I wasn't sure if that made me happy or upset.

Lizzy stirred in the little bed next to mine. I waited to see if she would fall back to sleep. When she started to fuss, I climbed out of bed to comfort her. I picked her up and carried her to the big bed and climbed in next to her. I snuggled her little body close to mine. I loved her with all my heart and being. She was perfect. Devin had given me the best gift in the entire world. It was impossible to hate him when he'd given me something so beautiful.

"Shh, baby girl, Momma's got you," I whispered, kissing the top of her head.

She was soon fast asleep. I loved that I had the power to comfort her, to make her feel completely safe and at ease in her little world. I wanted that feeling. I wanted someone to cuddle me and make me feel better.

"It's going to be okay," I murmured. "Momma will fix this."

When I'd made the decision to come back to New York, I had thought I was coming to save the family business. I was willing to put in the work to pull it back from the brink. I wanted to save it for me and Lizzy. I had some grand ideas of me and her working in the company together. We were going to be a powerful mother-and-daughter team and were going to rule the city.

I had been naive and foolish to think I had that kind of power. For the second time that night, I had been shown just how insignificant I truly was. I wasn't a badass. I didn't have any power. Devin had shown me that.

I closed my eyes and tried to quiet my mind. I hadn't slept much at all the night before. I *had* to sleep. I couldn't be off my game. I needed all my faculties about me. I was going up against sharks, and I didn't know if I believed Devin when he said he would walk away. I didn't trust him as far as I could throw him.

I was quickly learning a lot about what I truly wanted for my future. I had been working hard at the firm in California, learning new tricks and gaining valuable experience. I had planned to use all that experience to better myself. I thought I was positioning myself to take over the family business. Now I knew there wouldn't be a business in five years. Hell, there probably wouldn't be a business in a year.

"What a mess," I whispered, running my fingers through Lizzy's silky hair. "We'll go home soon. Mommy will fix this, and we'll never come back."

I was glad she had no idea about what was going on or what I had done. I would walk my father through the rest of the negotiations. I would make sure the contracts were signed and the deal was done. When it was all official, I was hopping on the first plane back to California, and I didn't plan on looking back.

I could admit that part of me dreamed of a future with Devin. Despite all the horrible stuff that had happened between us, I'd always believed there was something there. I thought with some time and distance, he could learn to forgive, and we could move forward. I knew I was to blame what happened. I had lied to him. I had deceived him. I had never gotten the chance to explain to him why I did what I did.

I felt like I was mourning a loss—a loss of something I never technically had. My future with Devin was officially a pipedream. Tonight was the final nail in the coffin. My heart felt broken for me and my poor little girl that would never know her daddy.

CHAPTER 13

DEVIN

I was in the worst mood of my life. I was pissed at everything. My coffee had tasted like shit, which damn near ruined my day. Everything was wrong. I wanted to break things. I wanted to smash everything in sight. I wanted to rage and scream and expel the sour feeling making me ill.

I punched the keyboard much harder than I needed to. I pulled up the chart I had been studying all morning. My brain was broken. I couldn't see straight. I looked at the numbers, looked at the projections, but it didn't make sense. I was usually sharp-witted and could quickly look at a chart and know right away whether it was worthy of my time that wasn't the case that time.

I clicked the mouse, wincing in pain. I looked down at my bruised knuckles and shook my head that had been one of many stupid decisions I had made in the last twenty-four hours. Last night, after crawling into bed naked, I thought I could sleep. I had been wrong. I had grabbed the bottle of whiskey from downstairs with the intention of getting shit-faced and passing out.

At some point, I'd punched a hole in my bedroom wall. I couldn't even remember the exact thing that had set me off. I knew it had something to do with Elly. As if the sore hand wasn't enough to make me regret my night, the fucking hangover was kicking me in the balls. I had thought about skipping work, but the last thing I needed was to be stuck at home and stewing on the matter.

Seeing my knuckles reminded me I needed to call my housekeeper. "Anna," I said when she answered her phone.

"Good morning, Mr. McKay," she replied.

"Can you call a contractor to patch the wall in my bedroom?" I said, hoping she didn't ask what happened.

"Yes, I will. Anything else?"

I cleared my throat. "Be careful when you go into my room. There's glass on the floor."

"I see. Anything else?"

"No," I answered. Then I thought about it. "I don't know."

Anna let out a long sigh. "I'll check."

"Thank you, Anna. I'll add a bonus to this month's check."

"Is everything okay?" she asked.

I smiled. Anna had been my housekeeper for years. "I'm okay," I assured her.

"Okay. Take care of yourself."

"I will," I said and hung up the phone.

I rubbed my temples, feeling a little guilty about the mess I had left Anna. The dinner had been left on the dining table. I wasn't usually a slob, but last night had been anything but ordinary.

"Mr. McKay." My assistant's voice floated through the intercom.

I sighed before pushing the button. "Yes?"

"I know you said you didn't want to be disturbed, but there is a Toby Michaels on the phone. He's persistent and says he needs to talk to you."

"Put him through," I told her. I needed to put that situation to bed.

The phone beeped once before I picked up. "Mr. Michaels," I said in a friendly tone.

"Toby, please," he said.

"Hi, Toby. What can I do for you?"

"I wanted to check in and see how things were going with the negotiations between you and the Savage firm," he said.

"Well, as it turns out, we have reached an agreement."

"Oh! That's good, right?"

I didn't say what came to mind. It wasn't good for him. "Yes, I believe so."

"Should I schedule a meeting?" he asked.

"No need. I'm going to be withdrawing my offer and because it wasn't official, you don't need to do anything. The Savages will likely be reaching out soon to go over the terms of their offer with you."

He was quiet for a second. "Oh. I'm sorry to hear that."

"Hey, it's not a bad thing," I assured him. "Your start-up is going to get the funding you need. You're set."

"I suppose I am, but I was looking forward to working with you, and learning from you. I'll be honest, I've done my research and I've been impressed with what I've seen. Your firm has done some great things for start-ups like mine."

I smiled, feeling a sense of pride. "Thank you." I had

to be the bigger man. I realized there was still a chance Toby could reject the Savages' offer that would not be good. Elly would blame me. She would be convinced I had something to do with the pullout. I sucked up my pride, knowing I had a chance to do the right thing. "You are in good hands with Elly Savage. She is one of the smartest people I've ever had the pleasure to work with. She's savvy and will make sure you're taken care of. I have personally worked with her. In fact, she interned for me a few years back."

"Really? I had a feeling you two didn't like each other."

I laughed. "No, not it at all. A little friendly competition is what you saw. You should feel good you had a couple of the big dogs fighting over you."

He chuckled. "I suppose you're right. Thank you for showing interest. Maybe there will be something we can work together on in the future."

"I hope so," I told him. "You have my number. Call me if anything comes up."

I ended the call, carefully cradling the receiver before I cursed a blue streak. I felt like I had just sucked on twenty lemons. I couldn't believe I had just promoted the Savages; it made me sick to my stomach as if the day couldn't get any worse.

I wanted a drink. Hair of the dog sounded like a very good idea just then. I sat back in my chair and rubbed the heel of my hands against my eyes. I hated being hungover; it was just adding insult to injury.

I debated calling it a day. I could tell my assistant I was working from home, but I couldn't go home. Anna was there. She would give me a look that was essentially wagging her finger at me. I heard my cell phone chime. I reached for it and saw it was a text message from Wes.

I opened it up, expecting an update on the business. It was a picture. I smiled as I zoomed in on the image of his pregnant wife, Rian, and their daughter, Ronny. They were standing on the edge of the family's boat with fishing poles in hand. Both mother and daughter were smiling for the camera. Wes had changed for the better since he had reunited with Rian. I envied him. I couldn't help but feel a little jealous. He had everything I had wanted. Wes was a good guy, but I didn't necessarily think he was any better than I was. I didn't think I was a bad man. I didn't screw anyone over. I donated a shitload of money to a variety of charities. I didn't break the law.

What the hell was so wrong with me that Elly couldn't seem to see me for the man I was? She looked at me like I was the devil himself. I wondered if that was how she viewed all her competition. Were they all unworthy of her because they were her father's direct adversary? I doubted it.

Instead of bellyaching about my lack of a love life and ignoring my friend, I quickly texted him back. I let him know he had a beautiful family and wished him good luck fishing. I put the phone back on my desk and turned my attention back to the computer screen.

I couldn't help but pull up the file for Toby's business. It was a damn good deal. I could have done some serious work with it. I could have made Toby a very wealthy man while providing a service that would benefit a lot of people. It just wasn't meant to be.

I realized now that my whole revenge plot had been a disguise for what I really felt. I was carrying a torch for Elly. Revenge gave me something to focus on. It gave me a place to put all of my feelings. I had been lying to myself. I knew my plan would likely lead me back into her life. It was all I had to hold on to.

I could only blame myself for what had happened. I had purposely put myself in her path, gotten the touch I wanted. Touch a flame and you get burned. I got burned. I had thought I could somehow exorcise the woman from my life if I could make her feel as bad as she'd made me feel. But I was wrong. Instead, I'd buried myself inside her warmth and set myself up for another, harder fall

I had to accept the possibility that I was not meant to have the kind of happiness Wes had found. Maybe I was a selfish, self-serving prick who didn't deserve the love of a good woman. I was thirty-eight and single. I had never had a serious relationship and honestly that led me to believe that I was the problem.

I stood up from my desk. I needed to get out of the office. I grabbed my phone and wallet and headed for the door. "I'm leaving for the day," I said to my assistant.

Her mouth fell open as her eyes went to the clock. "Okay," she said, not pointing out the early hour. "Should I forward your calls to your cell?"

"No."

She nodded. "Got it. Have a good day."

I walked out, anxious for some fresh air. I needed to walk. It was then I knew exactly what I needed. I climbed into the waiting town car and let my driver take me home. Once home, I went upstairs and changed into my swim trunks before heading to my private pool in the basement. Swimming always made me feel better. I did lap after lap, feeling the stress fade away. The fog of the hangover subsided, giving me a chance to think a little more clearly. Elly was not mine to chase. I was done with my need for revenge. It wasn't going to make a difference. Ron would destroy his company without my help. It was too bad really. Elly could have done great things with the company if her dad would have stepped aside. He'd been the master of his own destruction, and I just was lucky enough to get a front-row seat to see it all go down.

I wasn't sorry. Ron was getting what he deserved. If Elly was truly working for another firm and making a life for herself in California, she would be okay. Daddy's money would be gone, but I had a feeling she would make her own fortune one day.

I climbed out of the pool and grabbed my towel. As pissed off as I was at the situation and Elly's role in the whole thing, I was damn proud of her as well. It was the way I always felt when I thought about Elly—torn. She turned me inside out.

CHAPTER 14

ELLY

I had one of my favorite power suits on today. It was the typical severe black with a white blouse that had ruffles at the sleeves. I liked the way it fit me. I wore my favorite black pumps as well. I had taken extra time getting ready for the meeting, needing the boost to my morale. I believed in the theory that if you looked good, you felt good.

I smoothed the skirt down before taking a seat at the conference table. I pushed aside the thought I had sat in the exact same seat the last time I had been at the table. Devin had sat across from me, looking handsome as ever. It had been the beginning of what turned into a series of horrible mistakes.

Toby Michaels sat down at the head of the table. He looked a little nervous. I offered him a smile. "How are you?" I asked.

"Good, good," he said, nodding his head.

"Are you ready to do this?" I asked him.

"Yes, absolutely."

I pulled the file folder from my briefcase and slid it

across the table. "We've got the contracts ready for you to sign. They are the terms you and my father discussed."

Toby opened the folder and pulled out the first page of the contract. I watched as he carefully read through the paperwork. It was all pretty standard stuff, but I appreciated that he was a careful man. I glanced across the table to gauge my father's mood. He'd been chipper this morning when I met him at the office, but now he looked anxious. I watched as he loosened his tie. He was staring at Toby like he wanted to shake him.

"The terms are exactly what we talked about," my father blurted out. "I wouldn't try and slip anything in there."

Toby looked up from the paperwork. "I need to make sure everything is as it says. I don't sign anything until I read it."

"Good," I told him, trying to diffuse the tension that had begun to ramp up. "That's a smart thing to do. I do it as well."

Toby nodded, but his eyes were on the papers. I saw his brow furrow and knew something wasn't okay. Without looking up from the paper, he asked my dad a question about the fine print. I waited, letting my father field the question. He was hedging, not really answering the question at all.

"Will you be on the board?" Toby asked my dad and then me.

I shook my head. "No, I personally won't."

"I thought you were going to be a part of this?" Toby asked.

I cleared my throat, feeling a little hot under my collar. "No. I don't involve myself in the day-to-day stuff," I told him. "I'm only here to make sure the contract is complete and both sides are getting a fair deal."

"You deal with me," my father blurted out. "I'm the one that put this thing together."

Toby tapped the pen against the paperwork. "And will you be on the board? Will you be getting quarterly reports?"

My dad shrugged. "I trust you to handle your business."

Toby let out a breath before putting the pen down. It was a clear signal. My father's face turned red. I gave my father a look, telling him to keep his mouth shut.

"Toby, do you have reservations?" I asked.

"I do," he answered. "I'm a software engineer. That's what I do. I'm a businessman second. I was hoping that I could count on my investors to be a little more hands-on with the business side of things."

"I'm not going to run the business for you," my father snapped.

"Dad, he's not saying that," I told him. I turned to Toby. "What can we do to make you feel more confident with this?"

"I want to know how much support I'm getting. I understand you're investing money, but what else?"

I looked to my father. He visibly relaxed, and the man I remembered emulating when I was growing up appeared in the conference room. He put on the smile that had wooed many people over the years. "Toby, you and I have talked a lot about what you need and what my firm can do to make sure you get what you need. I will be there along the way. I will hold your hand through every step. I've been doing this for a long time. I have taken blossoming start-ups and turned them into Fortune 500 companies. You can trust my experience."

I watched as my dad picked up the pen and put it back

in Toby's hand. Toby hesitated for a moment. I could see him swaying. He was second-guessing the deal. I sent up a silent prayer. I needed him to sign. I couldn't leave New York until he did.

Finally, Toby let out a long breath before signing. I could tell he wasn't excited about it. I hoped he would feel better once things started rolling. My dad beamed, reaching over to pat Toby on the shoulder.

With the contracts signed, I quickly separated the copies, leaving Toby with his and sliding ours into an envelope. "Thank you, Toby. It was nice to meet you, and I wish you lots of luck."

I shook his hand and left the conference room. My father followed behind me. We stepped outside, and my dad fist-pumped the air. "Good job!" he exclaimed.

"What now?" I asked him.

He grinned, rubbing his hands together. "We sink the last of our assets into the start-up. Once the IPO goes through, we sell our shares and make a small fortune. It will put us back in the black. It will give the capital I need to start looking for new investment opportunities."

"You're going to turn around and dump it?" I asked, aghast.

"Well, yes. I don't have the liquidity to stay invested in a company that may or may not take off in the next year or two."

"I thought this was a long-term investment?" I questioned. "You stand to gain a lot more if you leave your shares alone. Selling them too soon shorts your profit."

He shrugged. "I need the money now. This was never meant to be something I was tied up in for more than necessary. I need the money. I thought I made that clear."

"But Dad, you just promised him you would hold his

hand through the IPO," I reminded him.

"I told him what he needed to hear," he replied. "You know how these guys get. It's going to work out great for him."

I closed my eyes, praying for patience. "Do you at least have a team ready to get him going in the right direction?"

My dad laughed. "A team? I'm it! I'm barely covering the expenses as it is."

I ran my fingers through my hair. "Who is going to put this thing together? You just had the man sign a contract that you can't fulfill."

He waved a hand through the air. "I've got an old friend who has a son that just graduated from business school. He costs me next to nothing to employ. He'll take care of all those little details."

"Little details!" I exclaimed. "Dad, that man trusted you. He trusted me! What did you do?"

"Don't worry about it. All we have to do is move some money around and get it set up. Any first-year business student can do that."

I shook my head. It was pointless to try and talk to him. He wasn't going to get it. All he saw were dollar signs. "You're going to ruin this," I said with exasperation. "It's another deal you're going to ruin. You are shorting yourself. You're going to let Toby down. He is a good guy. He sensed you were going to leave him hanging, and you are."

"Don't worry about it. If his stuff is as good as he claims, he'll be fine."

I wanted to walk away. I wanted to throw my hands in the air and just give up. My father was a lost cause. He continually disappointed me. "He isn't going to be fine. *You're* not going to be fine. You're going to burn through the very minimal profit you get from this deal. Leave the investment. Let it build. The payout is going to be worth it in the end."

He shook his head. "You're not listening to me. I'm on the verge of bankruptcy, Elly. I can't have all my money wrapped up in a single investment for months or years. How am I going to keep a roof over my head? I need the money. Once I'm set again, I'll be able to make those investments that reap big rewards."

"But you told him you were going to," I groaned. I wanted to stomp my foot and protest what he was doing. "Don't you understand what will happen to your reputation if you turn around and dump this? You will never be taken seriously again. No one will ever accept you as a legit investing firm. It isn't just your name that you're tarnishing—it's mine!"

"Relax," he spat.

"I can't relax," I told him, realizing it was pointless trying to make him understand. He wasn't going to get it. I didn't think he ever had. It certainly explained the current financial situation of the company.

"I need to go," he said, not the least bit bothered by my concern.

I watched as he walked out and hailed a cab. I couldn't remember him ever hailing a cab. He got in and left, leaving me standing on the sidewalk. Once again, he left me holding the bag. He had made a colossal mess of things and was in far deeper than I had thought. It was too much for me to fix.

There was only one person who could salvage the situation. It was the one person I certainly never wanted to see again, and I was pretty damn sure he felt the same way about me. I wasn't sure he would be willing to help. I laughed to myself. That wasn't true. I knew without a doubt he wouldn't want to help. He would laugh in my face.

I closed my eyes, then opened them and stared up at the gray sky. I was torn between walking away and just letting the chips fall where they would or fighting to save the deal. If it had been just my father falling on his face, I would probably let it go. I would see it as justice for all my dad's swindling, but it wasn't just my dad that was going to fall on his face. Toby would be left hanging. There was a chance he could recover, but not without some loss. The chances of him being able to attract another investor would be very slim. His company would be seen as a risk.

I liked the guy. If I would have kept my ass in California, I had no doubt in my mind Devin would have secured the deal and this wouldn't be happening. Devin was damn good at what he did. He was the kind of guy that could make diamonds from coal. Toby would be set for life with Devin's guidance.

I sighed, feeling disgusted with myself all over again. Toby wasn't set because of me. I had shown up to save the day and ended up fucking over the poor guy who'd gotten caught up in a war he had no idea was being waged. Toby was collateral damage in my father's eyes. I didn't see it like that. I actually cared about the people I did business with.

My conscience wouldn't let me leave it as it was. I was going to have to suck it up and make the call. Talk about eating crow. I didn't even want to think about what he would say when I asked for help. I was sure there would be laughter followed by very specific directions on where I could go. I had danced with the devil twice and come out relatively unscathed. I supposed a third tango couldn't be any worse.

I stepped forward and raised a hand to hail a cab. "Here goes nothing," I mumbled, dreading what was to come.

CHAPTER 15

DEVIN

I was still in a foul mood, but I wasn't ready to smash things. The swim had helped and a decent night's sleep had helped. Not drinking a bottle of whiskey had also been beneficial. I had told myself it was about staying on track. Proving I was better in every way by being successful. When Ron's company crumbled to ash and mine rose higher and stronger, Elly would see what she had missed out on.

Assuming she gave two shits. No more. No more thoughts of Elly. I had to let it go, for my own mental health. I focused on a small software company that I had found during my search. It wasn't quite as promising as Toby's, but it had potential. I had already started putting together a portfolio for it, and once I had all the information, I would decide whether it was a good investment.

"Sir," my assistant buzzed in.

"Yes," I answered, reminding myself to be nicer than I had yesterday.

"Elly Savage is here to see you."

I stared at the black phone. I had to have misheard her. "Who?" I questioned.

"Elly Savage," she repeated. "She says it's important."

I was certain we had nothing more to say to one another. Although, I was intrigued by her unexpected visit. The fact she was there meant it was something big. "Send her in," I said. If I refused to see her, I looked like a coward. I reminded myself she was dangerous and to not believe a word she said. She was the enemy.

I didn't bother standing up when the door opened. We were long past formalities. I barely looked at her. I did notice she was wearing a skirt that showcased her perfect legs and flat stomach. The shirt with the ruffled sleeve cuffs added a touch of femininity that looked good on her. She'd also taken the time to style her hair and was even wearing makeup.

"To what do I owe the displeasure?" I asked.

"I deserved that," she said sounding exhausted.

"Yes, you did. Why are you here?"

She sat down without being invited. It was pretty clear neither of us was interested in pretending to be polite. "I have a proposition for you."

I rolled my eyes. "Haven't we already done this? I'm pretty sure I know how this ends. Sorry, not interested."

"You've made it very clear you're not interested in mixing business with pleasure," she said, her voice lacking the usual biting tone. "I'm not here to offer you that. I'm here to offer a strictly business deal."

I stared at her, wondering what the hell her game was now. "In what world would the two of us ever work together? Do you honestly not remember the last few encounters we've had? Is this another one of your games?"

"No," she answered.

I shook my head. "Why me? Why are insistent on fucking with me? Literally and metaphorically."

"Devin, I'm not fucking with you. I'm serious."

I cocked my head to the side and studied her expression. She was lacking that usual fire. She actually looked almost humble. "You need my help to salvage the mess your father made," I stated.

Her eyes met mine. I felt that goddamn tug I had hoped to avoid. Her innocence did me in every damn time. She slowly nodded. "Basically, yes."

I blew out a breath. "What do you need from me? Keep in mind, I'm not feeling charitable at the moment."

There was a small smile that tugged at the corner of her lips. "Of course not. I would never ask for charity. I'm desperate, but not that desperate."

I smirked and nodded, signaling for her to go on. "We signed the contracts with the software firm," she started. "It wasn't until after the deal was official that I learned my father plans on having some kid fresh out of school put together the public information packet."

"You were fresh out of school when you worked on a pretty big deal," I reminded her.

"That was different," she said.

I smiled. "Because you have a knack for this kind of thing."

She offered a dainty shrug. "My father's firm has lost the bulk of its staff. There isn't anyone there to put together a lucrative package to take the company public and make the shares worth buying. I don't have to tell you what that will mean to not only our firm but Toby's business. This thing will never get off the ground."

I slowly shook my head. I hated that she was being dragged down by him. No matter what happened between us, I wasn't interested in seeing her fail. "I know."

"What?" she asked, her brow furrowing. "What do you know?"

"I know your father is basically the last man standing at his company. I know he's lost everything and is standing on a sinking ship and he was the one that drilled the holes. He never had the capital to invest in Toby's company. He might be able to offer a small infusion, but it's essentially plugging a bursting dam with a finger. It's all going down."

Her face fell. I nodded. "Let me guess: your dad got the deal. He's dumping the last of his cash reserves into the company, and he is hoping that by the grace of God, he gets it to go public. The moment it does, he wants to cash out and take the tiny little profit he might make and leave Toby holding the bag. Does that sound about right?"

Her head dropped as she stared at her hands in her lap. "You knew?"

"I take it by your sudden appearance in my office, you didn't?"

She looked up at me and slowly shook her head. "I didn't. I swear, I had no idea. I didn't ask enough questions. I assumed my father was prepared to shepherd the company into the big leagues. He promised Toby he would hold his hand through the process. I had no idea he was planning on cutting bait."

I believed her. I shouldn't have, but I did. "What do you think I can or will do? You pushed pretty hard to get that deal. You pushed me out of it."

"I did, but I think Toby is a decent guy, and I think his software could really be useful. He has what it takes to be the next Microsoft. He just needs the right team behind him."

I smiled. "And you think that's me?"

She winced. "I think if you would be willing to lend us your public offering team, we could get the jump start needed to launch his company."

I mulled it over. "You want me to give you my team of aces for what exactly? What are you offering?" I let my eyes drop to her breasts before meeting her eyes again. She squirmed in her seat, which was exactly what I wanted to happen. I had no intention of sleeping with her again, but I liked making her uncomfortable. Lord knew I had been in a state of discomfort for years.

"A partnership?" She said the words as a question.

I leaned back in my chair. "I liked Toby," I said, speaking my thoughts aloud. "I think he is a brilliant software engineer, and I do like what he has done so far. I think with the right tools and people working for him, he could definitely be one of the big players in the industry."

She slowly nodded. "But?"

"I am interested, but I'm only interested if I'm in charge. We do this my way. I will not attach my name to the Savage name if he's running the show. I don't trust him, or you, for that matter. I don't want my good name tangled up with the Savages, especially when your father's company goes down in flames."

Her eyes narrowed, and for the first time since she'd walked through the door, I saw a spark of life. "Trust me, the feeling is mutual. What are your terms?"

"I'll need some time to review the information. I had only preliminary numbers and projections and had planned to go over them once my deal was signed. I'll map out a plan. All parties will benefit. I am not doing this out of the goodness of my heart. I will expect a return on my investment."

"That is acceptable. I am not asking you to donate your time or your people. This will be beneficial to all involved."

I scoffed. "Some more so than others."

"You're right, but this is about Toby's company. I look forward to hearing from you and will do my best to keep an open mind. However, I too am not interested in charity. This needs to be mutually beneficial. After all, it is the Savages who hold the contract."

I chuckled. "As flimsy and worthless as it may be in the Savage hands." I saw her reaction and the hurt in her eyes I held up both hands. "Sorry. No more digs."

"You sure? Got any more in there you need to get out so we can get down to business?"

I smiled. "No. I'm good."

"Good. I look forward to seeing what you can do with this."

"It will be you and I working this," I stated. "I will not work with your father. The only reason I'm agreeing to any of this is because I like Toby."

I thought I saw hesitation on her face. I wondered if she actually thought she could set the thing up and hightail it back to California. There was no way in hell I would ever be in the same room with Ron Savage if I could avoid it. In this situation, I could avoid it. I held the cards. I could walk away and let it all crumble around them.

"I understand. Thank you."

"I'll be in touch," I said, getting to my feet.

She stood and paused. It would be weird to shake hands. Instead, she turned and walked out. I couldn't keep myself from taking a long, hard look at the body that had been naked and writhing underneath me on my marble floor. The door closed and she was gone.

The emptiness in the room felt as big as a black hole

without her presence. I hated that she could walk into a room and make it feel full. Her absence left an emptiness I couldn't quite explain. I rubbed a hand over my face. After all my protesting and vows to never deal with the woman again, I was right back in bed with her.

I knew she could have asked me for anything, and I would have agreed to it. I could talk a big talk when I wasn't looking at her. The moment she turned those blue eyes on me, I was putty in her hands. I had a feeling she knew it. Thankfully, she was kind enough not to rub it in my face. I was sure she wanted to and probably would once I saved her father's ass again.

CHAPTER 16

ELLY

I arrived at Devin's office a few minutes earlier than he had asked. I was taking the deal seriously and wanted him to know I was a professional. It helped if he could look at me like a business associate instead of a woman who'd slept with him to get what she wanted. Although that wasn't the case at all, I knew that's what he believed.

I was directed to go into his office without his assistant escorting me. That seemed to be a step in the right direction. Before, I felt like the woman was ready to tackle me to the ground if I stepped out of line. I had no doubt about my reputation in Devin's firm. Everyone knew who I was and likely had a general idea about what had happened years earlier.

"Good morning," he greeted from the sideboard in his massive office.

"Good morning," I answered, taking in the relaxed look on his face and his attire. He'd removed his suit jacket and skipped a tie. The top couple of buttons on his dark gray shirt were undone and the sleeves rolled up.

"Can I get you a drink?"

I raised an eyebrow. "It's a little early, isn't it?"

He laughed and shrugged. "I was asking if you wanted water, coffee, juice?"

I wasn't sure how to handle him being nice. "No, thank you," I answered. "We can work over here." He gestured to the seating area that was nothing more than two chairs and a small round table between them. It was one of the things that hadn't changed about his office.

I sat down, glad I had worn my black slacks. I didn't want to worry about keeping my legs crossed and knees together. Devin sat down, a bottle of juice in his hand. "Did you get the file?" he asked.

"I did," I said, pulling the printed version from my briefcase. "It looks fair to me. I'd like to go over the initial projections if that's okay. I'm worried we might be selling more than Toby can do."

He shrugged. "I pulled up the information he provided along with a current list of ideas he has in the pipeline. Some of the programs are very innovative, and I think if he can pay to get the right programmers in there, it will happen."

"You looked at his R and D list?"

"Of course. You didn't?"

I smiled, forgetting how thorough he was. "I scanned it, but I did not do a lot of research into the programs."

"I have my team going over the current stuff in development, the products he's already released, and some things other companies are working on. They'll put together a list of top three programs that should be pushed to the top and marketed to potential shareholders."

I nodded. He had covered a lot of ground in very little

time. "Who has final approval on what these top three are going to be?" I asked, testing to see if he was completely pushing me out of the loop.

"Ultimately, Toby."

"What does that mean?"

He shrugged. "I will, of course, have a say in the matter. I have a good instinct when it comes to knowing what will do well right out of the gate."

"I'd like to be involved in that decision process as well. I've been working in LA and have a pretty good understanding of what is happening out there. We are close to Silicon Valley."

He smiled. "That works for me. I wasn't sure how hands-on you would be in this."

"I will be. I'm not going to let this fall apart. It's why I brought it to you."

He nodded. "Okay."

"Now, what about the start price?" I asked.

He grinned. "You don't like what we've put together?"

"I do, but I worry it's too high."

He picked up the file from the table and opened it up. I watched him read through it. He was so smart and really did know what he was talking about. I did trust him when it came to things like this. He had a head for business and was a genius compared to my father. Hell, he could run circles around my dad. He *did* run circles around him.

I admired him. I always had. I hated what had happened between us. Once I realized he wasn't the villain my dad had made him out to be, I had felt tremendous guilt about my role in the whole situation. I wished I could take back what had happened. I would have loved to have a real relationship with him. He was someone I could learn from.

Not to mention, my daughter would have a father. But right now, with his animosity still so close to the surface, I couldn't risk him knowing about her.

"You're right," he said after several minutes. "I'll talk to the team. We should bring it down at least two percent. Any lower and we undercut what we are trying to market as a premium product."

"I agree," I said, pleased he was taking my suggestions.

He smiled and it felt like I had been washed in a warm ray of sunshine. He was handsome in the traditional sense, but there was something else about him I was drawn to. I loved his mind. He was brilliant, and when he spoke, you could hear the confidence in his tone. It wasn't condescending; it was reassuring. He would have made an excellent preacher or cult leader. People would follow him into the fires of hell if he asked them to. I had a feeling that was one of the reasons my father hated him. Devin was everything my father wasn't but wanted to be.

"You've done a lot with this in a short amount of time," I told him.

He shrugged. "I already had some of the work done. It was just a matter of pulling it all together."

I smiled. "Of course you did. This is going to be a great investment. I am confident the turnaround is going to be good for all of us. I guess the short-term investment plan isn't necessary."

He smirked. "A long-term investment is a short-term investment gone wrong."

I laughed—actually laughed. "I'm going to grab some water if that's okay," I said, getting to my feet. As I walked past his chair, he reached out and grabbed my hand.

It was a totally natural move for a couple. But we

weren't a couple. I looked at where his hand was on mine, his fingers around my wrist. My eyes moved to his. He looked just as shocked as I was. He released my hand, but I didn't pull mine away. His eyes dropped to my mouth. He was going to kiss me. I wanted him to kiss me. I debated bending down to take the kiss, but before I had a chance to move, my phone rang.

I blinked, pulled out of the moment. It was a good thing, I told myself. Kissing him would lead to much more. That would lead me to walking out of his office feeling like complete shit again. "I better get that," I breathed.

He nodded. "Go ahead."

I pulled my phone from my briefcase and saw Jane's number. "Hello?" I answered, turning my back to Devin.

"Hey, I'm sorry, are you still in your meeting?"

"I am. What's up?" I asked, turning back to Devin with my hand over the speaker. "I need to take this."

"Please, go ahead."

I stepped away from him, going into the corner of the office for some privacy. I couldn't step out and have his assistant eavesdrop. "What's going on?" I asked.

"Well, I don't want to freak you out, but Lizzy has a little fever."

"What is little?" I pressed, wondering if she was getting her molars and running a low fever. That would be normal

"I took it about twenty minutes ago. It was 101."

"What?" I gasped with alarm.

I turned to look over my shoulder. Devin was trying to look like he wasn't listening, but he was. I couldn't ask Jane the questions that were on the tip of my tongue.

"She doesn't seem too sick," Jane quickly said.

"I'll be there in about twenty minutes," I told her.

"I can handle it. Should I give her Tylenol?"

"No, I'll be there," I said and ended the call. I turned around and walked back to grab my briefcase.

"Everything okay?" Devin asked getting to his feet.

"Um, yes, fine, I need to go, though. I like what you've got so far. I'll be in touch."

"Friday?" he said.

"Yes," I answered, trying to hide the panic in my voice. "Friday at Toby's."

"I'll see you then," he said.

I rushed out of the office. I tried not to be one of those moms, but I couldn't help but worry about my baby girl. She was my everything. I told myself it was just a fever, probably something she picked up on the plane. I hated flying. I always felt like I was swimming in a pool of germs. Lizzy was never sick. I was very lucky to have a healthy baby.

A fever wasn't a big deal, I told myself as I hailed a cab. "She's fine."

She likely just needed her momma. We'd have some soup and ginger ale and veg out on the couch watching *Paw Patrol*. I would know more once I laid eyes on her. I got out of the cab and rushed inside. When I walked into the apartment, Lizzy was sitting on Jane's lap, cuddled up under a blanket.

"Hey, guys," I said, dropping my briefcase and going straight to Lizzy. "Are you sick, baby?"

"I don't feel good," she pouted.

I put my hand on her forehead. She didn't feel too hot, but her cheeks were red. "Let me get you some juice," I told her.

"She seemed fine when I got here," Jane commented.

"It could be molars. Did she throw up at all?"

"Nope. We played with the LEGOs I brought over, and I noticed she was kind of down."

"Thank you for the LEGOs, by the way," I said, opening the orange juice and pouring it into her sippy cup. "Here you go, sweetie."

I sat down on the other end of the couch. Lizzy climbed off Jane and into my lap. I snuggled her warm body against me, wrapping my arms around her and wishing away her ailment.

"How was your meeting?" Jane asked.

"Good. Great. It actually went really well. I did not think it would, but he was nice. He's got a great plan, and I think everything is going to work out just fine. My dad will be saved, and I can rest easy knowing the new company will be in good hands. I can go home and move on with my life."

"Are you sure that's what you really want?"

"Yes," I answered without hesitation. "No good can come from me hanging out here. I need to go back before things get really complicated."

Jane looked at Lizzy and smiled. "Yeah, I could see how things could get messy."

"It's better this way," I insisted.

"I know," she said. "I know."

She got up and collected her things. "Get better, kiddo. We've got big plans to hang out again soon," she said to Lizzy. "I'm sorry, but I don't do puke or diarrhea. If that happens, you'll need to call a real nanny."

I laughed. "I wouldn't leave her if she was actually sick. And one of these days you will have to learn to deal with the puke and poop."

She grinned. "Nope. I'll hire a slew of nannies."

I shook my head. "You say that now, but when your

precious little angel is the one spewing, I bet you'll be right there to take care of it."

She grimaced. "I don't think so. Not in a million years."

"See you later," I said as she walked out of the apartment.

CHAPTER 17

DEVIN

I slid the tie around my neck before quickly tying it without thinking about what I was doing. It was second nature to me. I straightened the power blue tie before adding my tie clip. I reached for the jacket that matched the black pants. As usual, my tie was the only splash of color in my outfit. I turned left and right in the mirror, making sure I looked good before heading downstairs.

I couldn't believe how nervous I was about the meeting with Toby and Elly today. I had gone through similar meetings hundreds of times. I had the experience. I had the knowledge, and I knew my proposal was good. Yet, I was acting like a newbie, fresh out of school and meeting my first client.

The reason wasn't hard to figure out. It was the fact I was seeing her. Things had been going so well between us at my office the other day. I couldn't believe how well we'd been getting along. It had been like old times—the times when I didn't know she was acting as a spy. She'd been nice, friendly, and her smiles were genuine. It had been easy to have a conversation with her. For a brief moment, everything had been right in my world. It was as if I had stepped into a parallel universe, one in which she and I were friends.

I had let myself believe we had turned a corner in our relationship, that there was a chance we could be friends. Then it came to a grinding halt the second her phone rang. I had been seconds from pulling her into my lap and taking what I craved. The phone call had been strange. She'd really been concerned about something. The immediate change in her easygoing attitude told me it was something big.

I had to consider the fact she had a life in California. That life very likely included a boyfriend. The thought of her with another man made me furious. Jealousy flooded my veins, followed by white-hot anger. The thought she was toying with me while some poor sap sat back in LA waiting for her to return did not sit well with me. I didn't think she was the kind of person who would cheat on her boyfriend, but what did I really know about her? She'd fooled me. Maybe her boyfriend was just as blind. She was very skilled in the art of deception. I had to acknowledge that everything I knew about Elly Savage had been a cover. She had been lying to me from the very first moment we met.

"You'd best remember that," I mumbled to myself. I couldn't get caught up in another one of her schemes. I didn't think I would recover a second time.

I walked out of the house to the waiting car. It was time to focus on the deal. I wanted Toby to know he was going to get everything he needed to take his company to the next level. I knew he was nervous about it. He'd held off going public for a long time. My research revealed he'd been approached last year but rejected all offers, claiming he didn't think it was the right move for the budding company.

I liked that he wasn't the kind of guy to make rash decisions. That was going to be important in the months and years to come.

I walked into the building and was immediately escorted to the conference room. Toby rose to his feet from where he'd been sitting at the table. "Devin! I'm so glad to see you."

"I'm glad to be here," I told him, shaking his hand.

"I can't tell you—I probably shouldn't tell you—but I'm really happy to have you and your team on board. I was a little nervous when I was signing what I consider to be my life's blood over to a company I wasn't totally confident in. I'm looking forward to what you've got planned."

"I'm sorry there was some confusion in the beginning. We've got it all worked out now though."

"Thank God," he said with relief in his voice. "This is something that has kept me up for far too many nights. I feel like I'm hiring a nanny or something. This company is my baby. I'm glad it will be in your capable hands."

"I'm glad to be along for the ride. I reviewed all your files, and I'm excited to see what you've got in the works. As long as you keep doing what you've been doing, slow rollouts and paying attention to every detail, it's going to be a successful journey."

Our conversation stopped when Elly walked—no, breezed, into the room. I couldn't take my eyes off her. I didn't care if she had a boyfriend back in California. I didn't care if she had twenty boyfriends. I was going to look my fill while she was in front of me. She was in another one of her chic business suits that was sexy, powerful, and projected confidence. I could smell her perfume, something light and airy and so damn sexy.

I liked it. It was tickling my fantasies to life. I couldn't let my want of her get in the way. I had to keep my head in the game and out of the clouds.

"Hello," Toby greeted her. I stood as well, offered a nod before returning to my seat. I couldn't risk touching her. I knew the electricity that zinged between us would be obvious to Toby. I didn't want him to get the impression there was anything going on between us.

"Gentlemen," she said with a smile. "Sorry about my tardiness."

"You're perfect." I said the words before I had a chance to think about it. "Perfectly on time. I was a little early."

She smiled at me, warming me from the inside out. "Good to know."

I watched as she took her seat across from once again. The tone of the meeting was much different than the first time we'd sat down at the table. She seemed to be in good spirits.

"Thank you both for meeting with me," Toby said. "I appreciate all the time you have both put into this."

"You're welcome," we answered at the same time before we both gave small laughs.

"You've had a chance to review what Devin's team put together?" Elly asked Toby, getting right to the heart of the matter.

Toby nodded. "I have. I have a couple questions about the rollout and who will be appointing the board of directors."

I looked at Elly and gave her a slight nod, telling her to explain it to Toby. It was ultimately her deal, and she deserved to get as much credit for it as possible. She offered me another smile before turning her attention to Toby. It was well worth letting go of the reins to see her face light up.

I watched her talk, listening to her explain the details in a way that was easy to understand. She was thorough and knew her stuff. Anytime she mentioned something, she referred to it in the package of paperwork. I was mesmerized by her. A gorgeous woman that understood and spoke my finance language was the total package. She was amazing. I couldn't help but think she had been created and put on the earth just for me.

She was supposed to be mine.

Toby looked over at me, as if he was verifying everything she said. I needed to back her up. "Elly is exactly right. I told you, you are in good hands with her." I looked to Elly and smiled at her. "You've said everything I would have said."

Elly blushed a little. "Thank you. I'm here to answer any questions you have, Toby. I'm sure there will be things that come up along the way. You have my cell. You can call me day or night, and I'll do what I can to answer. If I don't have the answer, I will get it for you."

Toby nodded. "Thank you for walking me through all of it. I'm sorry to be a pain in the butt about it."

"You are not being a pain at all," she assured him. "You have questions, and that's a good thing. It tells me you care about the company, which is going to be another selling point."

"When does this all happen?"

"Well, I think we're almost there. Things are moving fast. We're working on creating some buzz. Don't be alarmed if the shares don't sell like hotcakes the first few days or even weeks. This is a marathon, not a sprint."

"You guys both seem pretty confident," Toby commented.

I smiled and nodded. "I certainly am. I'm thrilled to be a part of this."

"I am as well," Elly answered.

Toby nodded. "I think I'm ready. I've waited a long time for this. I was reluctant to go public, but after a lot of consideration, I know it's the right thing to do."

"It's a big step, and I definitely understand your hesitation," Elly told him. "We'll do all we can to ease the growing pains that are sure to come. It is difficult to give up control of something you've built with your own two hands. Just remember to keep your eyes on the prize."

Toby nodded, taking a deep breath. "It is my biggest concern, but with the wording in your contracts, I'm confident I'll be able to navigate it just fine."

We chatted a bit more about what he expected. Elly answered his questions with patience. I was impressed, absolutely impressed with how far she had come in so little time.

"If that's all, we'll get out of your hair," I said to Toby.

"That's all I have."

"My team will be in touch next week with finalized plans," I told him.

"It was nice to see you again," Elly said.

We walked out of the conference room together. I stopped Elly just before we got to the door. I had to give credit where credit was due. "You did great in there," I told her. "You put him at ease, and I can see he really respects you and trusts you. That isn't something that comes easy."

"I appreciate that," she said with a friendly smile.

"You deserve it."

"Thank you again for agreeing to do this."

"You're welcome," I told her.

I opened the door for her and let her go first. I wasn't

ready for our time together to end. I figured since we were getting along so well, I may as well ask her to lunch. The worst she could do is shoot me down. Before I could ask her, I noticed something behind her. Not something—someone. I inwardly groaned as Ron Savage barreled down the sidewalk.

"Fuck," I muttered under my breath.

"What's wrong?" Elly asked. She turned to look behind her. "Shit," she breathed.

There was a young guy trailing behind Ron, who was moving much faster than I thought was possible for a man of his girth. With the look on Ron's face and Elly's sudden change in demeanor, I had a feeling shit was about to hit the fan.

Ron came to a halt in front of us. His cheeks were flushed, and his eyes were flashing with anger. "What the hell is that asshole doing here?" he seethed.

Elly looked up at me, an apology in her eyes before she turned back to her father. "We've been working together on this deal."

"What?" he snapped.

She sighed. "He's helping us get the IPO set up."

Ron glared at me. "He has no business here!"

I opened my mouth to reply but quickly shut it when Elly shot me a look. It was her party. I had no idea what was going on, but I was going to guess Ron didn't know I was involved. Elly had kept him in the dark? I wasn't sure what that meant, but I was going to be very interested to find out.

If there was any double-dealing going on, I was going to lose my damn mind.

CHAPTER 18

ELLY

I couldn't believe my father had shown up. He was going to ruin everything. I had planned to explain what I had done, but I wanted to wait until everything was completely tidied up. I knew there was a chance he would puff out his chest and do exactly what he was doing.

He was pissed. More pissed than I had ever seen him. The last thing I needed was for him to try and start shit with Devin. Devin was not a man to back down. The two of them had been circling each other for years. It was a lit match hovering over a pile of dry straw. If there was a brawl, it would ruin our credibility. I wouldn't blame Toby a bit if he decided to pull the deal, no matter what it cost him.

I stepped in front of my father, trying to block his view of Devin. I knew it wasn't possible, but I wanted his attention on me—not Devin. Honestly, Devin would shred him given the opportunity. I couldn't blame him for wanting to go after my father. Not really. My loyalty was to my father, but he had been a scoundrel. He would have screwed over Toby, himself, and ultimately me. I hauled my ass out to

New York, did something I wasn't proud of, and he was going to destroy everything I had worked for.

"Dad, what are you doing here? How did you even know I was here?"

He glared at me. "I didn't know you were here!" he snapped. "It appears I arrived at just the right time. I get to see your betrayal with my own two eyes! The better question is what are you doing here with him? He's our enemy!"

I rolled my eyes. "Nobody is betraying anyone."

"Not this time," Devin muttered behind me.

"We don't have any enemies either. This isn't the Dark Ages."

"Speak for yourself," Devin mumbled under his breath.

I turned to shoot him another look, asking him to keep the comments to himself. He barely looked my way. His eyes were locked on my father like a tiger locking his gaze on a juicy T-bone steak. "Again, why are you even here?" I directed the question at my father. "You said you had a meeting today."

My eyes went to the young man standing behind him. The kid actually had pimples on his face and looked like he was playing dress-up in his daddy's suit. The poor guy was looking at me and Devin with fear and confusion. I wondered if he was my dad's assistant. My dad couldn't afford to pay an actual professional. It made sense he would hire a kid fresh out of high school.

I watched him straighten his tie and jerk his chin up. "I came by to introduce my new VP to Toby. I wanted to see how things were going, check in with the guy. I told him I would keep in touch, and I always follow through with my promises."

Devin's loud choking sound was very deliberate. The tension between them ratcheted higher. I needed to defuse the situation before it came to a head and the police were called. The last thing either of them needed was to be arrested on assaulted charges.

I sighed. "You don't need to worry about any of that," I told him. "I've got everything taken care of. I told you I would handle it. I'll set up a meeting with you tomorrow and go over all the details."

He scoffed. "Oh, I can see that. You went running to Devin McKay for help. What did you tell him?"

Before I could answer, Devin stepped forward. "You're damn right she did, and it's a good thing she did. You were dead set on bungling another deal. It's all you know how to do. It's a miracle you still have a company."

"You shut your mouth." My father seethed. "This is none of your business. This is mine! My deal! You are not going to worm your way in on this. You think you can flash your smile and wear your expensive suits and woo anyone. I've got news for you, not this time. Your flashy looks aren't going to keep you going forever."

Devin chuckled. "My flashy looks are doing just fine. And, it is my business."

"No, it isn't. Elly and I got the contract. Your name is nowhere on those documents."

Devin turned to look at me, questioning me. I winced, knowing Devin was about to tell my father exactly why it was his business. He was going to enjoy the telling of it as well. There was no stopping it now.

"You may have gotten the contract, but I'm the one doing the legwork," Devin started. "My company is getting a share of the profits because of my contribution. I'm paying the IPO team—you are not. I'm making sure this is worthy of my name being attached to it. You damn well better believe I'm going to make sure there is a profit to make. I'm not backing off this time. I'm in this, and I will not be withdrawing."

"What the hell is he going on about?" My dad turned his furious gaze on me.

I shrugged. "I had to do something. Your shortsighted plan wasn't good for anyone. We needed a team to put together a package that would entice people to buy shares. I needed help."

"And you ran to him," he growled.

"I made an agreement that will be beneficial to all parties involved," I said, barely keeping my cool. "I needed Devin's expertise and experience."

"What am I, chopped liver?"

I heard Devin's guffaw and had to fight to hold my own in. "Dad, this is a fair deal. Toby is very happy with the package we've put together. He's completely on board with it. The best part is you are going to make a lot more money than if we would have stuck with your idea. This is a win-win. You'll have the capital to keep investing and build up the company again."

His lip curled, his face turning a deep shade of red. He did not look well. His hands curled into fists as he stared me down. "Bullshit! I will not stand by while this man tries to steal this deal out from under me. I found this investment opportunity. He's trying to cash in on my hard work! He thinks he can steal another deal from me! I'm not letting the little thief get his hands on it!"

He sounded ridiculous. I had a very good understanding about why Devin did not like him. He was acting like a childish fool. I was embarrassed for him. I was embarrassed for me as well. "He—" I started to argue but Devin stepped forward. His broad shoulder blocked my view of my father, forcing me to step to the side.

Devin was a commanding force. He towered over my father, and the lanky child playing with the big boys was no match for Devin in any way. "I'm not a thief," Devin hissed. "I don't steal. Ever. I only play fair."

"Bullshit!" my father spat. "You wouldn't know fair if it bit you in the ass."

I winced, hoping Devin had a cooler head than my father. "I've entered into a legally binding agreement. Elly came to me. Toby is on board with what I've put together. This deal will go through, and it will be my way."

My dad shook his head. "No, it won't."

Devin gave an incredulous laugh. "I don't know who you think you are, Ron, but this deal is done. I'm involved, and I'll be damned if I let you get mixed up in this and fuck it up. That's what you do—you fuck things up. You don't know the first thing about how to make money. You sure as hell can't keep money. Let Elly and me handle this and sit back and count the profit that falls into your lap. Watch me do what I do and think about how much better I am at doing it."

"Nope, I don't think so," he replied with a smug look on his face.

Devin's deep, sinister laugh had me on edge. I could see him barely restraining himself. My father kept poking him. Someone should have told him never poke an angry bear. "I'm not wasting any more of my time discussing this with you. It's well in hand. Scurry off and go see what else you can screw up for your daughter to fix."

"You won't have a damn thing to do with this deal. You'll walk away from this deal, just like you walked away from your daughter."

I froze. My mouth fell open. I quickly snapped it shut to

keep from throwing up all over Devin's immaculate Italian leather shoes. "Dad!"

Devin looked at me with confusion and then back at my father, who was grinning. "Run away. That's what you do best. I'm going to tell Toby and everyone else what kind of man you are. You walk around like you're king of the world, but you're a piece of shit that deserts his own kid."

"What the fuck are you talking about?" Devin hissed.

"Dad, shut up!" I protested, silently hoping the sidewalk would open up and swallow me.

"No, I won't keep my mouth shut any longer," my dad said, clearly realizing he had just found a thread to pull that would get to Devin. "What will people think of you when they find out you knocked up your twenty-one-year-old intern and then left her alone to raise the baby without giving her a damn penny."

"That isn't what happened," I argued, my voice lacking any real authority. Everything was happening too fast.

Devin was looking at me with confusion, as if he didn't understand the words that were being spoken. When it dawned on him what my father was actually saying, his confusion morphed into anger. He glared at me with such fierceness I actually recoiled.

I turned my own anger on my father. I stepped forward and shoved his shoulders, pushing him back several inches. "Go! Get out of here!"

"That man doesn't get to get away this!" he protested.

"Go!" I shouted. "You're making a mess of things." I shoved him again.

"God dammit, Elly!" he shouted.

"Go home!" I yelled.

"I'll go," he groused, waggling his finger at me, then

Devin. "This isn't over. It isn't over by half. I'm going to get my money."

He turned to his new VP and grabbed his arm, pulling him down the sidewalk. I almost asked him to come back. I suddenly didn't want to be alone with Devin. I could feel the anger radiating off him. I dreaded what was coming. It had been almost three years in the making. It was time to face the consequences of my decision that had been made in haste.

I closed my eyes, gathering the courage to face the man. I turned and found myself taking a step back. He was beyond furious. I had thought I had seen him pissed before. What I saw on his face in that moment was so much more than anger.

"Devin—" I stopped. I didn't know what to say. There was nothing to say. My dad had said it all.

CHAPTER 19

DEVIN

My head felt like it was stuck in a beehive. There was an intense buzzing in my ears. Initially, I thought Ron was drunk, confusing me with himself. He said "your daughter." I thought maybe he meant *his* daughter. It hadn't occurred to me he was actually telling me I had walked away from my own daughter. How could it?

His words replayed on a loop in my head. I watched as Elly shouted at him to shut up. She'd been horrified when he'd kept talking. That should have been the point where I realized Ron was speaking the truth. Sadly, my sluggish brain didn't pick up on it until the man was walking away. He said Elly had gotten pregnant with my child? It couldn't be. It didn't make sense.

But it made *so* much sense.

It explained her vanishing from New York. It explained why she never took my calls and why I never saw her at any of the functions I knew her father would be at. I had purposely gone to parties and benefits the Savages often attended. She had never been there; it was like she'd fallen off the face of the planet. I told myself her disappearance was the result of her shame.

I looked at her, searching her face for an explanation. I silently begged her to tell me her father was making it all up. Ron was wrong. I wasn't the father. She had a boyfriend and he was the child's father. I stared at her so hard, willing the truth to surface.

The longer I looked at her, I realized I was in for a hell of a day. The guilt and worry on her face made it evident that it was true. I was a father. I felt like I had been kicked in the gut by a steel-toed size fourteen.

"Elly?" I breathed her name.

"Devin," she said, shaking her head, tears in her eyes.

I looked up at the sky before looking into her blue eyes. I had once believed she was innocent. Those angelic features were her disguise. She was the proverbial wolf in sheep's clothing. The longer I looked at her, the angrier I became. She had lied to me over and over and over. I wasn't sure she had ever told me the truth in all the time we had known each other. She was a habitual liar.

"My daughter?" My throat felt raw.

"I can explain," she blurted out.

I laughed. "I don't think you can."

"Please, let me explain," she begged.

"You..." I seethed. "I can't." I shook my head. "Not here."

I grabbed her arm and walked down the sidewalk, heading for my waiting car. I yanked open the back door before giving her a gentle push into the back seat. I had to make a conscious effort not to manhandle her. She was a woman—the mother of my child at that, apparently.

"Devin." She said my name again.

"A daughter?" I snapped.

"Where to, sir?" the driver asked.

I ignored him, staring at Elly. "What the hell is your father talking about?" I demanded. "Why would he think I knocked you up?"

"Should I head to the office?" the driver asked, clearly uncomfortable with the situation.

"A daughter!" I shouted, not bothering to answer the driver.

Elly blurted out an address, ignoring my demand for answers. I was struggling to make sense of everything. My brain was going in a thousand different directions. Images of a pregnant Elly popped into my head. Had she truly had a child? I thought back to the frantic round of sex on my foyer floor. I noticed no changes in her body, but that didn't necessarily mean anything. I hadn't noticed much of anything except what it felt like to be consumed by her wet heat.

The car jerked forward, snapping me back against the seat. It was the jolt I needed to pull me back into the moment. I was spinning. My brain was going about a million miles an hour. I pictured the child she gave birth to. I couldn't make sense of it all. Did the kid have blonde hair? Did she look like Elly? What was her name?

They were questions a father should be able to answer. The word felt foreign, like it didn't belong in my vocabulary.

I turned to face her. "Elly, is it true? Do you have a daughter? Do I have a daughter? Am I a father?"

She slowly nodded. "It's true. I do have a daughter."

I put a hand over my face. I couldn't look at her. "What the fuck?" I breathed. I didn't miss the part where she said *she* had a daughter. That was too much for me to try and dissect in the moment. I told myself to put a pin in it and circle back to that little detail.

"I didn't mean for you to find out like this," she replied.

I pulled my hand away and looked at her. "What you really mean is you didn't mean for me to ever find out. That's why you moved across the country."

She shrugged. "Yes. I moved because I wanted a fresh start. I didn't want to complicate things any more than they already were."

"You wanted a fresh start with *my* child. You didn't answer me; were you ever going to tell me about her?"

She turned and looked out the window. It was the answer I had expected. I cursed, turning to look out the opposite window. It was too much to take in. I was out of my element. I could handle a stock crashing, a company executive arrested for fraud, or losing a multimillion-dollar deal. A secret child was not in my wheelhouse.

"I honestly didn't think I would ever see you again," she said in a soft voice. "I didn't think you would ever want to see me again after what happened."

I turned to look at her, studying the features I had committed to memory. None of it was real. Everything I thought I knew about her was a lie. "Is your name really Elly?" I asked.

"What?" she asked, wrinkling her nose. "Of course it is. Don't be ridiculous."

I shrugged. "It isn't ridiculous, not when you consider all that you've told me, or not told me. It's stupid to ask. You wouldn't tell me the truth anyways. You seem to be pretty good at making things up as you go. You have a knack for deception."

She blew out a breath. "I didn't lie to you."

"You had my child!"

"Yes, I did, but I didn't lie to you. I didn't tell you. That is very different."

"Ever heard the term lying by omission? That's what you did. You lied. And you kidnapped my child now that I think about it."

She frowned at me. "I didn't kidnap anyone. She's my child too."

"I underestimated you. I thought I had you figured out. The betrayal was one thing, but this, my God, this is next-level. You are, I don't know what the hell you are, but I hope you're proud of yourself."

"You're making it sound like I purposely got pregnant. That isn't the case at all. Trust me, it was as much a surprise to me as it is to you now. I was twenty-one and pregnant by a man that hated me. I wasn't exactly thinking straight."

I had to look away from her. I was so pissed I couldn't stand being near her. I had no words to express my anger. I was afraid to put words to my emotions. I didn't want to say something I regretted later. As furious as I was with her, she was the mother of my child.

Holy shit. Just thinking those words boggled my mind. A child. Me. A father. It made no sense. The child would be two now. Two years. What did she look like? I had so many questions. Unfortunately, I couldn't put them into words.

"Devin, I know you're angry, and I can accept that," she said. "Despite your anger and what has happened between us, it doesn't change the deal we have. We can take this IPO to the market and follow through with our promise to Toby. Once it's done, I'll leave. I'll go home."

"You'll leave," I repeated. "Just pick up and go home. You expect everything to go back to normal?"

"You'll never have to worry about seeing me again," she said. "I'll be gone."

"Again," I snapped.

"I just need to see this through. I have to make sure my father's legacy is safe. This deal is too important to let fall apart now."

I couldn't believe how cold she was. She didn't seem to give two shits about turning my life upside down for a second time. She'd just exploded my life and she wanted to talk business. I couldn't do it. I couldn't think about deals and IPOs. I could barely remember my name.

"Are you serious right now?" I asked her.

She nodded. "I am. This is important. This deal is everything for my dad's firm. Without it, he loses everything."

My eyes widened. "He loses everything? Are you honestly asking me to put aside everything I'm feeling right now so your daddy doesn't go broke?"

"It's business," she stated. "You of all people know business isn't personal."

I shook my head. "Only you would think that. My business is personal. I take it all personally. Maybe that's something you need to learn."

"My father's livelihood depends on this deal going through," she insisted.

"I don't give a fuck about your father. This is about me, us. Our child."

"Devin, I need you to understand this deal is important. That's what matters right now."

The car pulled to a stop. I looked at her, trying to figure out what to say to her. I felt like I was talking to a stranger. She wasn't the woman I thought I knew, not even the traitor I knew her to be. The woman I was looking at was someone else entirely.

"What matter is us," I told her. She bit her lower lip, her

eyes glassy and sadness on her face. "Devin, there is no us," she whispered.

Before I had a chance to respond, she climbed out of the car and raced down the sidewalk. I watched her move but didn't bother to chase her. There was no point. I had no words. I needed some time to process it all. She disappeared inside a building at the end of the block.

"Sir?" the driver said.

I looked at him. "Just drive," I told him.

He gave a slight nod. There was no doubt he had overheard the conversation. The car pulled into the street and blended into traffic. I felt numb. I felt like I was floating, looking down at my life from somewhere else. I felt disconnected.

My analytical brain took me back to the beginning. I had to start from the top and work my way through the problem. I fast-forwarded through the part where she'd pretended to be a naïve intern and skipped to the night in my office. I didn't think either of us had expected it to happen. She might have been trying to seduce me, but that night had felt spontaneous.

Spontaneous, which meant unprotected. I had just assumed she'd been on the pill. I didn't even consider the idea she could be pregnant. I was a grown man and should have known better. I felt responsible for getting her pregnant. I hated that I never got to take responsibility for my role in the situation. No wonder her dad hated me so much. I would hate me, too.

I wondered if he knew that I had no idea about the baby. What had she told him? Did she tell him I'd taken advantage of her and when she turned up pregnant, denied responsibility? Once again, I had more questions than answers.

CHAPTER 20

ELLY

I burst through the door, locking it behind me. I didn't know what I expected him to do, but the locked door gave me a sense of security. I had an instinctive need to protect my baby. I knew she wasn't in danger from him, but things were not good. Everything was falling apart.

I wanted to shield her from the shitstorm that was likely going to swoop into our normally mundane lives. All because I had come back to New York. I had been so close to securing my father's company, and now it was all hanging by a very weak thread. Things had been perfect and in the blink of an eye, shattered.

I wanted to shake my father for what he had done. Was he purposely trying to sabotage himself? He was destroying his future, and I couldn't seem to stop him. He was going to be a pauper. All the money my grandfather had saved was gone because my dad couldn't control his tongue. He was impulsive and never thought before he spoke. He acted without worrying about consequences. I couldn't understand how the two of us could be so different and still be related.

I walked directly to the kitchen and grabbed the bottle of wine from the kitchen counter. I poured a glass, trying to steel my nerves. My hands were shaking so bad I nearly dribbled wine down my chin. I cursed under my breath before taking another long gulp. I didn't day drink. I especially didn't drink when Lizzy was up and about.

"Um, do I dare ask?" Jane asked, coming into the kitchen, her eyes on the bottle.

"Where's Lizzy?"

"I just put her down for a nap. What happened?"

I groaned. "He knows."

"Who knows what?"

I took another drink of the wine. "Devin. He knows about Lizzy. He's so pissed. So, so pissed and I'm so, so fucked."

Her eyes widened. "What? How? You told him?"

"My fucking dad told him," I hissed.

"Grab your glass and come tell me what happened."

I carried the bottle with me and flopped on the sofa. "Devin and I had just gotten done with the meeting. It went great. Everything was so perfect. We were set to roll out next week. I was walking on air when I walked out of that meeting. We were talking and friendly, and I felt like we had finally turned a page in our relationship. He was so nice and respectful in the meeting. He made me feel like an equal. It felt so good. And then, my father showed up like hell on wheels. He started going off about Devin stealing the deal from him."

She nodded, encouraging me to continue. "Your dad has never liked Devin.?"

"Right, so I purposely didn't tell him about it because I

didn't want the two of them at odds while we talked with Toby. So, when my dad found out Devin was involved, he lost his shit. He started spouting off about Devin not getting a penny of the profits and on and on. When Devin let him know it was going to be done his way, my dad hit him below the belt. He took a great deal of pleasure calling him a piece of shit for knocking up his daughter and walking out on her."

Jane's eyes grew round. "Did you deny it?"

I rolled my eyes. "How could I? He wouldn't have believed me anyway. He really hates me now. And my dad. I don't even know how to help him. He's sabotaging himself. I had him squared away. He would have been set, but now, I don't know. Devin's smart. He can find a way out of this and take Toby with him."

"Would he do that?"

I scoffed. "In a heartbeat. He was furious."

Jane blew out a breath. "I hate to say this, but I think you have to walk away. You said it yourself, your dad is set on destroying himself. Save yourself and walk away."

I rubbed two fingers over my throbbing temple. "Maybe you're right. This whole thing is just a complete disaster. I should leave before Devin gets over the shock and starts plotting revenge like he did the first time he found out I betrayed him. He set out to ruin my father, and while I can't blame him entirely for how that worked out, he would have taken him down if my dad didn't do it himself."

"I'm sorry," she offered. "This really sucks."

"What if he sues me for custody?" I gasped, the realization that he could destroy the life I knew with my daughter slamming into me. I started to panic. My heart raced at the thought of losing my baby girl.

"Relax, you're getting way ahead of yourself. From what

I know about Devin McKay, the last thing he wants is a kid."

I shook my head. "He was furious with me. What if he does it just to hurt me? Would he stoop so low to use his own daughter as a pawn?"

Jane put her hand on my shoulder. "I don't know, but you have a lot on your side. You've been raising her by yourself this whole time."

"Because he didn't know. He's got more money than I do! He could destroy me in a long, drawn-out legal battle. I wouldn't be able to go back to California." I took another drink of the wine. Then another ugly realization stole into my brain. "Oh my God," I breathed.

"What's wrong?"

"My dad," I said. "He used me as a pawn in his war against Devin. He doesn't care about me. He *used* me."

Jane leaned forward and gave me a hug. "I'm sorry honey. It's okay. I won't let Devin get to Lizzy. I have more money than he does or damn close to it. I will hire you a whole team of lawyers to fight him. I will assassinate him in court if he dares fuck with you."

I couldn't hold back the laugh. "Thank you. You're such a good friend."

"Anytime," she said, patting me on the back. "I got you. If all else fails, I'll whisk you and Lizzy away on the family jet. We'll go somewhere tropical with no extradition policy."

I burst into laughter. "I'm a little afraid of you."

"Don't be. Just stay on my good side."

"You're crazy," I told her. The landline rang. I groaned knowing it was probably my father. "I'll get it," Jane offered.

"It's fine. I better get this over with before he shows up here. I don't want him upsetting Lizzy." I reached for the phone. "Hello," I answered with resignation.

"Miss Savage, it's Ernie, at the door. You have a visitor. Should I send him up?"

I didn't understand why he would be asking if he could send up my father. "My dad?"

"No, it's a Devin McKay."

My stomach dropped. It was stupid to have the car drop me off at my building. I hadn't been thinking clearly. There was no getting away from him now. "Yes."

"What's going on?" Jane asked.

"It's Devin. He's here."

"Want me to kick his ass out?"

I smiled, shaking my head. "I don't want to make it any worse."

"Are you sure?"

"I'm positive."

A minute later there was a knock on the door. Jane opened the door and stepped close to Devin. My friend wasn't exactly big, but her fiery red hair gave her just enough of a crazy look to intimidate people. I knew she would never hurt anyone, but the crazy ran strong in her. "You better watch yourself, mister. I've got your number. You hurt her or disrespect her, and I will make you pay in ways you didn't know were possible."

She turned to look at me, winked, and walked out. Devin walked inside and closed the door. "Nice lady," he muttered.

"She's a good friend looking out for me. She can be a little overprotective." He let out an audible sigh. The man looked beat. "Can I get you a glass of wine?"

"I think I need something a little stronger than wine."

I noticed his gaze scanning the apartment. I was suddenly embarrassed. There were LEGOs and various toys scattered about the place. I watched as he took in the scene. I was sure it was probably a lot for him to cope with. I understood that, but I wouldn't allow him to do anything I felt wasn't in Lizzy's best interest. Neither of us talked for several minutes.

"What are you doing here?" I finally asked when he didn't say anything.

Instead of answering, he stared at me. I felt like he was trying to see inside my head, like he had Superman vision and was analyzing me. The longer he stared at me, the more I freaked out inside. I didn't know what he was going to do. My mind automatically jumped to the worst-case scenario. My heart was pounding in my chest, and my palms were damp. I rubbed them on my thighs.

I couldn't take it anymore. The silence was killing me. I threw up my hands. "Just say whatever it is you came to say. Spit it out!"

He raised an eyebrow but said nothing.

"What do you want? Why are you here? If you're just here to insult me or taunt me, leave. I'm not interested in hearing any of it."

His mouth flattened into a thin line, but he still refused to talk. I was losing my fight. I couldn't keep doing it.

"Fine," I said, my shoulders sagging forward. "I'm making some tea. I don't have scotch or whiskey. Do you want some tea?"

I walked into the kitchen and filled the kettle before putting it on the stove with my back to him. I heard him walk in behind me. I fought to keep my hands from shaking. I turned on the burner and turned to face him.

"I thought you were drinking wine," he said in a low voice.

"I don't drink during the day," I retorted.

Once again, one of those dark eyebrows quirked upward.

"I had a few sips, that was it."

He stepped closer to me. He was absolutely invading my personal space. I could feel his breath brushing over my hair. I wasn't going to back down. I wouldn't be intimidated by him. I inched my chin up and looked him in the eyes, and I couldn't fight the little tug of regret I felt when I stood this close to him. I hated that things were such a mess between us.

I wished like hell things were different. I didn't have to wonder why things were the way they were. That was on me. I had made a series of choices that hurt him. I wanted to use the excuse I didn't know better, that I had believed my father, but it was flimsy. I was an adult. I could have made different decisions.

I didn't, and now it was time to own up to my mistakes. I would take the blame for what I had done, but I would not let anything happen to Lizzy. Her life would not be negatively impacted. I would do what Jane suggested before I ever let him take her from me or use her against me.

CHAPTER 21

DEVIN

My heart hurt. I had never felt such pain. It was the pain of betrayal mixed with something that went much deeper. I was still trying to put it to words. I was speechless and was even more confused about her reaction to my reaction. She acted like I had done something wrong. She was the one acting like the injured party.

"Devin, step back," she ordered.

It was yet another thing I couldn't understand. She acted as if I was an intruder in her life. In her daughter's life. *Our* daughter's life. The child was mine. At least, that's what she was claiming. Or not claiming. It was one of the many questions that was swimming through my brain.

"I need some answers," I told her.

"You haven't asked any questions."

"Don't push me away," I snapped. "You act as if I'm bothering you. I have a right to know."

"Know what?"

"Why?"

"Why what?"

I ran my hands through my hair. "Everything. Why everything. Why didn't you tell me you were pregnant?"

She blew out a breath. "Because I had just helped my dad steal that deal from you. Things had been kind of crazy, and I didn't realize I was late until after everything was said and done. I knew you were going to be furious when you found out."

"Obviously," I growled.

"Exactly. I knew you were going to be pissed. I couldn't walk into your office, where I was no longer welcome, I might add, and tell you I was pregnant."

"Yes, you could have," I told her, shooting down her flimsy excuse.

"Devin, would you have believed me?"

I shrugged. "I don't know."

"I don't think you would have believed me. You weren't exactly in a mind to believe anything I told you at that point."

I gave her a dry look. "I can't imagine why."

"Even if you believed me about the baby, then what? Do you think you would have wanted me or my daughter in your life?"

I shrugged. "I didn't get a chance to make that decision. I didn't get to decide what I thought about any of it. I deserved to at least have a conversation about it."

"I think you know how that conversation would have gone," she insisted. "You had just lost something big because of me."

I shook my head. "I don't have a clue how that would have gone. I can't say how I would have felt. You had my child. Do you understand what that means? *My child*. I'm not going to pretend I wouldn't have been pissed at you. I was and I still am. What happened back then was a shitshow."

"Devin, I truly, truly didn't know who you were when I went into that office posing as an intern," she insisted.

I held up a hand. "I'm not interested in getting into all of that. I can't deal with that right now. I want to know about the baby. I want to know how your father knew, but I didn't. What did you tell him?"

She made a face, shaking her head. "I made a lot of mistakes back then."

"Did you tell your father I knew about the pregnancy and rejected my own child?" I asked, the very words like a stabbing sensation in my gut.

"Not exactly," she hedged. "I told him you didn't want anything to do with me. I didn't specifically tell him it was your child."

I was still having a hard time wrapping my head around the whole thing. "But he guessed. Why? Why would he assume it was my child? Did you tell him?"

She winced. "No. Kind of. Things were so complicated back then. I was young and confused and just trying to do right by my dad."

"Adding the fact that I knocked you up to your father's long list of reasons why he hated me seemed like a good idea? You told him I took advantage of you?"

"I didn't have to tell him that. He figured that out on his own."

My eyes narrowed. "I did *not* take advantage of you. I'm not a monster."

"I didn't say you were."

"But you certainly didn't deny it when Daddy dearest found out his sweet little girl wasn't quite so innocent," I sneered. "Did it make it easier to paint me as the bad guy?"

"I didn't do that," she argued. "I was young and confused and terrified."

I ran a hand through my hair once again. "I could have helped. I could have offered financial support. That would have helped take off some of the burden. It was my responsibility to help. I'm a lot of things, and you can say what you want about me, but I never would have ignored the needs of my own child."

She shrugged. "I wasn't sure about that. I was financially independent and didn't need your money."

"But I could and should have been a part of the child's life," I insisted.

She cocked her head to the side, studying my face. "Have you ever thought about having children? Did you want children?"

"I'm not going to lie and say I wanted kids, but I don't know if you can say you wanted kids in that moment either, can you?"

"I was twenty-one," she said with a smirk. "I didn't know what I wanted, but I don't regret her for a second. I had to learn very quickly what it took to be a mother."

I slowly nodded. "Exactly. That's what you took from me. Maybe I didn't know what I wanted. You got the chance to have your mind changed. I didn't get that chance. I didn't get the chance to be a father and figure it out."

"Devin, I get it, but I knew you pretty well."

"And I didn't know you at all," I replied. "The man you thought you knew wasn't real. It was colored by who you thought I was based on what your father had told you over the years. It's no secret Ron and I go back a long way. I know he hated me long before you ever waltzed into my office."

"You did know me," she insisted. "The person you knew

was who I really was. My lie was *why* I was there. Everything else, that was me."

I rolled my eyes. "Elly, everything I knew about you was called into question. I questioned myself, my judgment. I thought about that night in my office and had to wonder if you purposely seduced me. Did you?"

"No!" she protested. "That was not planned."

"Are you sure? Was it your way of getting back at me? Were you hoping to learn about more of the deals I was working on?"

She shook her head. "I didn't plan on that happening. Whatever you think of me, I didn't intend to sleep with you that night. It just happened."

I took a second to digest what she had said. I couldn't help but think her plan had been to sleep with me from the very beginning. I had to tell myself to think the worst of her because every time I turned around, she was hitting me again with another lie or betrayal. I felt like I had been beaten repeatedly. I needed to guard myself against whatever else she was going to throw my way.

"Do you understand it's hard for me to believe anything you tell me right now?" I asked her. "I want to believe you didn't purposely steal away my child in an effort to hurt me further, but how can I not?"

The guilt on her face didn't make me feel any better. "I didn't do it to hurt you. I truly didn't think you would want anything to do with a child I was carrying. I expected you to tell me to get out. I expected you to laugh in my face when I said the baby was yours. Like you said, why would you believe anything I said at that point?"

"I'm not going to tell you I wasn't pissed. I was. I was furious with you, but you thought so little of my character that you felt it was best to never tell me about a baby I fathered? Why not tell me after things settled?"

She grimaced. "I didn't think little of you. It just seemed easier if I left town."

"I would have been there for you, for her," I told her, looking directly into her eyes. I said the words that tore at my heart. "What's her name? I don't even know my daughter's name."

"Lizzy," she said softly. "Her name is Lizzy."

"How old is she?"

"Just over two," she answered with a smile.

I nodded. It was more information than I had started with, but there were so many more questions. "I want to know her. I want to be a part of her life. I'm not going to accept no for an answer. It's nonnegotiable."

The teakettle started to whistle. She spun around and quickly turned off the burner. I didn't move. I wasn't about to back down. I had made up my mind in that moment. I was going to be in my daughter's life. If I had to get an entire team of lawyers involved, I would. She'd stolen two years from me, and I wasn't willing to settle for another two days lost.

She poured water into a cup before she finally turned back to face me. "I suppose you're right."

"You suppose? Elly, I want to see her. I'm not going to go away. You can't run back to California and hide from me. I will find you."

"Don't threaten me," she snapped.

"I'm not threatening you. I'm trying to make sure I have a spot in my daughter's life. Where is she?" I looked around, wondering why I hadn't heard her. Kids made noise. I hadn't heard a peep. "Is she here?"

"She's taking a nap," she finally answered.

"She's here?" I gasped. The idea I was in the same apartment with my child I didn't know existed was mind-blowing. I had to fight the urge to go find her. I was desperate to lay eyes on her. I wanted to meet my daughter.

"She's sleeping. Devin, this needs to be done right for her sake."

"Do you have a boyfriend?" I blurted out.

"What? What does that have to do with anything?"

"I want to know if another man has been raising my child. I want to know if she thinks of another man as her father."

She had a small smile on her face. "No, I don't have a boyfriend, and she has never been around a man."

That was oddly satisfying. "I want to see her."

"I understand. She'll probably sleep another hour, maybe two. She was sick—"

"What?" I asked with alarm. "The phone call. It was her."

She nodded. "It was just a little tummy bug. She's fine, but I want to make sure she gets plenty of rest."

"Okay. When?"

"How about the park tomorrow?" she offered.

I didn't care for a public meeting, but clearly, she didn't trust me. It was a little offensive, and I wasn't going to hide it. "You don't trust me?"

"About what?"

"You're arranging a meeting in public because you don't trust me to be alone with the two of you."

"No, I'm suggesting the park because she's been cooped up in this apartment and could use some time at the park. She'll be in a good mood and having fun."

I couldn't really argue with her. I didn't know the child. I didn't know what made her happy or sad. I didn't know what she liked and didn't like. I knew absolutely zero about my own kid.

"Fine. Don't pull any shit, Elly. I'll do this your way, but if you fuck with me, I will not stand by and let it happen. Not again."

Her eyes flashed with anger. "Do not threaten me," she warned again.

"I'll be at the park tomorrow," I said, shooting her once last look before leaving the apartment.

The moment I was away from her, I released the breath I felt like I had been holding since I had first heard about my child on the street. I knew it was going to take some time for me to get my head around it. First, I wanted to see Lizzy. Once I finally laid eyes on my baby, I could start planning my next move. And there would be a next move. I wasn't going to roll over and play dead for the Savage family anymore.

CHAPTER 22

ELLY

My eyes felt like sandpaper had been rubbed over my corneas. I could feel the puffiness under my eyes and hoped I didn't look like total hell. I had used some eye drops to hide the redness, but I knew my lack of sleep was evident. I hadn't slept a wink. My mind could really conjure up some wild scenarios given the chance. With a sleepless night with nothing to do but think, my brain took full advantage.

I didn't know what to expect from Devin. I was terrified he would try and get custody. I would not let it happen. I had no delusions that I would have to share her with him, but I wouldn't let him take her. I wasn't even sure he would want that, but I had to be prepared for anything. He would want to hurt me like I had hurt him. He would want to exact some kind of revenge. Taking my daughter would gut me.

He was a powerful man with means. That was a dangerous combination in an enemy. Jane's warnings had filtered into my subconscious, and I had decided at some point last night I would become a fugitive if that's what it took. I would not allow him to use my daughter as a pawn to hurt me.

I checked the time on my phone and scanned the park. I had shown up early, wanting to scope out the place. One of the many scenarios that had crossed my mind was that Devin would try to snatch my daughter. Rationally, I knew that was ridiculous, but I had come early, wearing a baseball cap pulled low over my eyes with dark sunglasses hiding my face. I had strolled through the park looking for police who might arrest me for kidnapping or hired kidnappers.

I was losing my mind.

My stomach growled. I had skipped breakfast. And dinner the night before. I was too worried to eat. I had debated jumping on a plane last night and fleeing the city. But I couldn't do that to him, me, or Lizzy. I wouldn't make her pay for my sins or the sins of her father. She deserved the chance to have a father in her life. If he walked away, that would be that. I would never let him toy with her or hurt her.

"Hi." I heard Devin's voice.

My head shot back as I looked up at him from where I was sitting on the park bench. I had chosen a bench away from the bulk of the other parkgoers, just in case things got ugly. "Hi," I replied. He was dressed in his usual expensive suit with a dark-colored shirt, minus the jacket. He was holding a stuffed pink-and-purple unicorn with a shiny horn. I immediately knew Lizzy would love it. "Is that for me?" I asked, trying to lessen the tension.

He looked terrified. "No, I uh... is it not age appropriate?" he asked. "The lady at the toy store told me it was safe for a two-year-old."

"It's perfect," I assured him, actually appreciating the gesture. "Have a seat."

He sat down, his eyes focused on Lizzy, who was sitting in the grass in front of me. "Is that her?" he whispered.

I smiled. "Lizzy, someone wants to say hi."

She popped her head up and immediately saw the unicorn. Her hazel eyes lit up as she got to her feet. She stared at the stuffed animal in Devin's hands. He was staring at her, not moving or saying a word. He almost looked afraid of her.

"Unicorn!" she exclaimed.

Devin nodded. "Unicorn. It's for you." He held out the stuffed toy, and she eagerly took it, snuggling it against her face.

"What do you say?" I prompted.

"Thank you," she answered with a big smile on her face.

"You're welcome," Devin answered.

"Play," Lizzy said, pointing to the playground.

"Let's go play," I answered.

She took off running for the playground equipment with her unicorn in hand. I followed behind her with Devin beside me. "Isn't she too little for that?" he asked with concern.

"She loves to slide," I told him.

He watched as she managed to climb up and run for the slide. She dropped to her butt and slid down the big slide, her face filled with joy. The moment her feet hit the soft rubber material below the slide, she took off running to do it again.

We watched her go down the slide a few more times without speaking. Lizzy tripped on her way back around. Devin sprang forward, walking across the padded playground, and helped her up. "Are you okay?" he asked her, brushing off her knees.

She looked at him like he was crazy. "Go more!" She grinned before running to the ramp to go up for another turn down the slide.

He followed her, watching as she walked across the wooden bridge to the slide's opening. He moved to stand at the end of the slide and reached down to scoop her up as she slid down. Lizzy squealed with delight, clearly enjoying the new twist in the game.

I watched the two of them play. Devin followed her around as she tried some new things. He kept his hands on her with the unicorn under his arm as she attempted the climbing wall. Watching the two of them together softened my heart toward him. I had expected him to be cold toward her, stiff, and the kind of guy that didn't actually want to hear or talk to his kid but just pull her out and dust her off when it was time to give his image a boost.

That wasn't the case at all. He was a natural with kids, it turned out. Some of the other kids on the playground asked him to push them on the swings. I couldn't help but laugh as he walked down the row of swings, gently pushing each of the children. They all squealed whenever it was their turn. I watched the other moms watching Devin. I knew exactly what they were thinking, and I couldn't help but feel a little jealous.

After a lot of swinging, Devin carried Lizzy on his hip back to where I was on the bench. "I should probably get her some lunch," I told him.

"Why don't we go across the street and grab a bite?" he suggested.

"You don't have something you need to do?" I questioned.

"Nope. I'd like to have lunch with my daughter."

"Okay, lunch it is." I packed up the diaper bag I still carried even though she didn't technically wear diapers.

Devin carried Lizzy as we left the park while Lizzy carried her unicorn. It had quickly become her favorite. I had a feeling it would be sleeping with her that night as well. It was thoughtful of him to bring her a gift. I was truly impressed and surprised at how attentive he was to her.

We got a table at the casual dining restaurant with Lizzy in a booster seat. I ordered her chicken pieces and fries and a burger for myself. I was starving, and now that the initial meeting was out of the way, I felt like I could relax a little.

"Does she eat by herself?" Devin asked curiously.

I shrugged. "Yes and no. I still have to cut her food and make sure she eats and doesn't just play with it."

He nodded, seeming to file away the information. When the food was delivered, he focused more on making sure she was eating than eating his own meal. I was actually able to eat my burger while it was still warm.

"Does she like ranch?" he asked.

I shrugged. "I'm not sure."

"Lizzy, do you want to try some ranch on your chicken?" he asked her. His voice was filled with excitement, making the idea sound enticing.

She was eager to do anything her new best friend asked of her. He showed her how to dip the chicken in the ranch before taking a bite. She intently watched him as he did it again, taking a bite of the chicken piece and making sounds of pleasure.

She grinned and grabbed her own chicken piece and copied him. When she obviously enjoyed it and went back for another, Devin looked at me. "You've never given her ranch?"

I shrugged. "It's not something I usually eat."

He frowned. "You can't eat chicken nuggets without ranch."

I laughed. "Ranch is messy."

We looked back at Lizzy, who had proven me right. It was all over her fingers and face. Devin grabbed a napkin and gently wiped the sauce away. "I've heard you can wash these things."

"Kids?" I asked with a puzzled expression.

He smiled. "Yes, kids."

I burst into laughter. Seeing him like this was making me rethink my decision three years ago. He was a good father, or at least, he would be given the chance. He was good with her. He changed when he was with her. The usual serious look on his face was gone. He looked happy and completely at ease with her. I had not expected it.

I watched the two of them talk about ranch. He showed her how to dip her fries in at as well, which rocked her world. I wondered if he had been right. Would he have been around even though I had betrayed him? Seeing him with her now, I had a feeling I had made a hasty decision.

I couldn't help but wonder how my life would have been different if I would have stayed in New York. If I would have told him about the baby. It had been a hard two years. Raising a baby on my own had been lonely, and there had been many nights I cried myself to sleep out of pure exhaustion. I realized now it didn't have to be like that. He would have shared the responsibility. He would have been there to support me and take her off my hands when I needed a break.

"Are you okay?" he asked.

I blinked. "What? I'm fine."

He gave me a nod before turning his focus back on Lizzy. I noticed he had barely eaten his own burger. She had captivated him. It was like there was nothing and no one else in the world just then. My heart squeezed as I realized I had been depriving my little girl of the attention from what was obviously a very doting, loving father.

I vowed to make it right. I didn't know where we went from there, but I would have to try and work something about with Devin. I owed it to her.

CHAPTER 23

DEVIN

I couldn't take my eyes off the little sprite. Her eyes were just like mine. Her fine hair was a dark blonde/light brown color that was the perfect combination of light and dark from Elly and me. She was the prettiest little girl I had ever laid eyes on and I was instantly in love with the child. I knew from the moment I saw her, she was mine. There was no way in hell I would ever leave her.

"Go ahead and eat," Elly said. "I'll make sure she finishes her lunch."

I looked down at my plate and realized I hadn't eaten. Elly's burger was almost gone. "You did this on your own," I said aloud, but more to myself.

She smiled. "I did. You learn to eat cold food, standing up, while vacuuming, or even showering if need be."

I nodded. I didn't like it. I could have been there. I could have shared the responsibility of feeding our child so she could eat, sleep, or even shower. It was hard not to be pissed. I was angry with her for taking my daughter away from me. She had stolen something that could never be replaced. A million sorrys would never make up for the time I had lost.

It wasn't like she apologized in the first place. She was still convinced she was in the right to leave town while pregnant and never tell me. I heard Lizzy giggle and looked over at the two of them. Elly was teasing her with a fry. She would pretend she was going to give Lizzy a bite before snatching it away at the last second and taking the bite herself. Lizzy clearly thought it was the funniest thing ever.

My anger softened a little when I saw the interaction between them. Lizzy and her mother were very close. It was evident in the way they interacted. What she had done was wrong, but I was grateful she had taken such good care of Lizzy. The child was well cared for and showered with love

"She's going to be ready for a nap soon," Elly said after our lunch was over.

I nodded. "Okay."

"You're welcome to come to the apartment if you'd like to help put her down," she offered.

"I will," I said, jumping at the chance to spend more time with her.

She smiled. "All right, Lizzy, it's time to go home. You need a nap."

"No nap," Lizzy pouted.

Elly didn't seem bothered by Lizzy's protests. Once again, I carried Lizzy on the walk two blocks up to the apartment they were staying at. I loved holding my child. It was oddly comforting. Her little head rested on my shoulder as we walked, and my heart nearly burst with love.

"She doesn't like to take naps, but she needs them," Elly said as we stepped into the elevator. "I need her to need them," she laughed.

"I get it," I agreed.

Once in the apartment, Lizzy seemed revived and ran around the place, picking up the various stuffed toys she had. I sat on the couch as she brought me each one. Every time she brought me one, I said something about it.

"She'll do that all day," Elly said with a laugh.

"How many does she have?" I questioned when my lap was filled with stuffed animals.

"Here, maybe ten or so. She has a giant tub full back home. I brought a couple with us, but every time we go out, she falls in love with a new one. I can't help but buy them for her. She's so cute when she asks. I know I'm spoiling her, and I'll probably regret it later, but not now."

I smiled, happy to know my daughter was spoiled. I would be spoiling her as well. Lizzy picked up one of the animals in my lap and carried it to Elly. I watched as Elly picked it up and wiggled it. "Lizzy, I'm sleepy," she said in a childish voice before nuzzling Lizzy's face with the stuffed bear.

Lizzy giggled and came back to take another one from my lap and carry it to her mother. It was a large black bear. "Let's take a nap," Elly said in a deep growl befitting the bear.

Once again, Lizzy squealed with laughter when Elly attacked her with the bear. For the next ten minutes, it was one toy after another from my lap to Elly's. Then, she reversed the game and brought each one to me. I realized I was expected to make the animals talk as well.

I played along until all of the stuffies were out of Elly's lap and back in mine. "All right, munchkin, it's time for you nap," Elly said.

"No," Lizzy protested.

"You can sleep with your new stuffy," she promised.

Lizzy snatched the unicorn from my lap and hugged it close.

"Where does she sleep?"

"I'll show you," Elly answered, picking up Lizzy and carrying her down the hall. There was a small bed in a corner with a soft pink blanket on it.

Elly laid Lizzy in the bed and pulled the blanket over her. She dropped a kiss on her forehead before standing up. I wasn't sure what I should do—or could do. I went with my instinct and copied Elly, dropping a kiss on Lizzy's forehead. "Good night," I murmured.

I watched her for several seconds. Her bright eyes stared up at me. I knew she didn't know who I was, but I hoped one day she would call me Daddy. Her eyes started to close, and I knew it was time to go. I wished I could have stayed and watched her a little while longer, but not just then. I needed to work out an arrangement with Elly and soon. I didn't want to miss out on any more time with my little girl.

I walked out of the bedroom with Elly behind me. She quietly closed the door before we moved into the living room. "You've done really well with her," I said.

"Thank you. She's a smart girl, and thankfully, she's a good girl. She's healthy and I feel very lucky to be her mom."

She was smiling as she spoke. There was a glow about her when she talked about Lizzy that I found irresistible. I couldn't explain why it turned me on to see her being such a good mother, but it did. I couldn't deny myself the chance to steal a kiss before I went.

I stepped toward her, my hand resting on her cheek. I used the pad of my thumb to rub across her cheekbone as I looked into her eyes. It was hard to believe the two of us had made a baby together. I bent my face toward her, waiting to see if she would stop me.

She didn't. Our lips barely touched. It never took much for that spark of electricity that always seemed to happen when I touched her to ignite a fire. My lips pressed against hers, demanding entry. She willingly opened her mouth, her arms going around me as I stepped closer to her.

My tongue plunged inside, sweeping over teeth and finding her own tongue to duel with. Her soft moan fueled the need burning low in my belly. My erection sprang to life. Anytime I was near her, my cock was always on high alert. My hands moved over her body, reaching around to grab her ass and pull her against me.

Both of us groaned in unison when my dick rubbed against her. I needed her as much as I needed the very air I breathed. I was guessing I had at least an hour before Lizzy woke up. I was going to use every minute of it. I wanted to savor her body. The only times we'd been together, it had been fast and furious. I had moved so fast I had no time to really enjoy her beautiful body.

"How long do I have?" I whispered, moving my mouth over her neck.

"Hour, maybe two," she breathed.

"She won't come out here?"

"No," she whispered. "But—"

I silenced whatever it was she was going to say with a kiss. I wasn't in the mood to hear excuses. I knew she wanted me as much as I wanted her.

"Bedroom," I said, asking and demanding at the same time.

"Can't. I share with her."

I silently cursed. Damn if I wanted to fuck on the carpet and risk rug burns. It didn't matter. All that mattered was me getting another chance with her. I pushed aside my disappointment at not getting to take her in a bed and focused on what I did have—her.

My hands moved to the light sweater she was wearing and pulled it up and over her head. I dropped it on the floor, stepping back to admire her. I reached for the bra, unhooked it, and slowly pulled it forward. Her full breasts with the pert nipples begged to be touched. I did so with my mouth. I sucked one nipple between my teeth, holding her breast in my hand. Her hands ran through my hair as her back arched, pushing her breast against my face.

Her hands moved to the belt on my pants. "No," I told her, pulling away from her and looking into her eyes.

"No?"

I gently pushed her hands away. "Not yet. I want to take my time."

Her soft smile sent a shock of heat through my body. "I like the sound of that."

I went back to her breasts, devoting a great deal of attention to each of them before I started to get a real kink in my back. I wasn't interested in standing up and making love to her. I undid the button of the jeans she was wearing and pushed them over her hips, taking the skimpy thong she was wearing with them. She stepped out of the booties she was wearing and kicked them to the side.

She stood before me completely naked. The feeling that stirred up within me was indescribable. I had seen her naked before, but this felt different. I traced my finger between her breasts and over her navel. I saw tiny marks low on her belly and realized those were signs of her carrying my child. Seeing them, touching the faded stretch marks, made me feel oddly possessive. My child had ridden inside her, stretching her body. I hated that I had not been able to witness the miracle.

My hand splayed over her now flat stomach before reaching around and pulling her close to me once again. My mouth covered hers, slowly exploring. I was hard and desperate for her. Her hands went back to my belt. I didn't stop her. I wanted to feel her silky-smooth skin against my own. The moment the belt was undone, her frantic fingers went after the button and then the zipper. I could feel her desperation in her jerky movements.

She pushed my pants open and without hesitation, slid her hand under the waistband of the briefs I wore. Her fingers caressed over my erection before wrapping her hand around me and tugging. "I need you," she gasped, the hunger in her voice nearly my undoing.

My patience had run out. My self-control faded. I needed her. Fuck taking my time. I was too desperate to be buried inside her. I yanked my shirt over my head, not bothering with the buttons. She was tugging my pants down. I managed to kick off my shoes and pull my shirt off at the same time without tumbling to the floor.

With both of us naked, I pulled her to the couch. I gently pushed her down, tugging her head to one end before climbing over the top of her. It wasn't ideal and the quarters were certainly cramped, but I didn't care. I was desperate for her.

I propped one elbow on the couch cushion, doing my best to keep from squishing her. I looked into her eyes, tracing my fingers over her cheek before trailing them down her neck and back to the breasts I decided I really liked.

They had been ignored our first two times together, a mistake I planned on never making again. I dropped my mouth to hers and kissed her, relishing in the feeling of our naked bodies pressed together. I would never get enough of the woman. I knew that deep inside my soul. She was mine.

CHAPTER 24

ELLY

He was being so gentle and slow. It had never been like that between us. I liked the slowness, but it was doing nothing to squelch the fire burning between my legs. I could feel his hard shaft pressed against my thigh. The limited space made it impossible for me to move. I was pinned against the couch with his naked body covering mine.

His hand moved to my belly. He seemed to have a new fascination with the region. I wasn't embarrassed by the stretch marks. They were marks I was proud to carry. His hand pressed against my stomach, warm heat from his palm infusing me. The hand slid to my hip before moving over my thigh. It was intimate, unlike anything we had shared before.

With my only free hand, I stroked down his back. I felt the rippling strength across his back, moving down his spine and sliding over his firm ass. The man was in excellent shape. I had never had the chance to ask him what he did to stay in such good shape. I certainly appreciated the effort he put into it.

I opened my legs as best I could, inviting him to touch me where I was so desperate for it. His hand slowly slid over the inside of my thigh before making its way up. I gasped, my eyes opening as I stared into his hazel eyes inches from mine.

"I love that you're so wet for me," he said in a raspy voice.

"You make me crazy hot," I answered honestly. I didn't care that he knew he had power over me.

We adjusted our positions with him sliding over me. My leg dropped off the couch, my foot hitting the floor as I opened my legs for him to take me. I reached up to my hand on his cheek like he was so fond of doing to me. His eyes were heavy-lidded and full of intensity as he gazed down at me. The man had a way of looking at me as if he could see right into my mind. It was intimidating and exciting to have him turn that full focus on me.

He probed at my opening with the tip of his swollen cock. I spread my legs a little wider until he found his target. He slowly pushed inside, stopping while my body stretched and adjusted to his girth. His eyes held mine with every inch he pushed inside. I couldn't look away. It was as if he was demanding I look at him without ever saying a word. I didn't want to look away.

He kept pushing inside me until he was seated up to his balls. The weight of his body inside me triggered a visceral response. I gasped, my eyes sliding closed as a wave of ecstasy rolled over me.

"Look at me," he whispered.

My eyes popped open. The intense stare made me squirm, heat pooling between my legs, flooding around him buried inside me. "Oh God," I whimpered. The sensations were unlike anything I had felt before. It was as if every nerve ending was being plucked and tweaked, sending juicy vibrations of sweet ecstasy throughout my body, inside and out.

I couldn't stop my body's response to his. The orgasm he triggered just by being inside me was more powerful than anything I had ever experienced. He watched me as I writhed under him, a low keening sound coming from low in my belly and escaping through my mouth that was partially open. My eyes were held captive by his. Him watching me while I climaxed was beyond intimate. It was the rawest and most vulnerable I had ever been with him.

When the climax finally released me, I reached up to him, putting my hands on either side of his face, and pulled him down to me. I kissed him passionately, infusing it with all the tenderness I felt for him in that moment.

His body began moving, sliding in and out of me, coaxing another orgasm from me before he finally gave in and took his own fulfillment. He fell on top of me. I wrapped my arms around his neck, holding him against me. I didn't want to let him go.

In that moment, I knew I loved him. I didn't know how or even why, but I did. I had loved him for years. Working alongside him had given me the chance to get to know him. I had fallen for him back then. That night in his office had been the best and worst night of my life.

"I'm squishing you," he said after a while.

I smiled, running my hand over his back. "Not at all."

He chuckled. "Liar."

He moved off me, sliding down to the floor with his back against the couch. I slid off and sat beside him. He put his arm around me and held me close. It was the first time we had the chance to enjoy postcoital bliss. It was strange but good.

"A bed would really be a good thing," I said on a sigh.

He looked at me and smiled before dropping a kiss on the tip of my nose. "I think we're doing okay without it."

"I suppose."

We sat in silence for several minutes. I liked that he wasn't racing out the door. There was something to be said for a little cuddling after sex. It made it all more meaningful and less about the act itself.

"I forgive you," he said after some time.

I looked up at him and saw the sincerity in his eyes. It was a big step in the right direction. "I forgive you too.""

I expected a smile. His face was anything but happy. "For what? What did I do that needs forgiving?"

"For trying to bankrupt our company and stealing the deal my dad worked hard on."

He looked confused. "Excuse me?"

"I had to fake being an intern to go to work for you to steal back the deal you stole from us," I answered.

His brows shot up. "What the fuck are you talking about?"

I pulled away from him, staring at him and trying to figure out why he was the one getting pissed. "You stole that deal my dad found. He had approached that company and convinced them to go public."

He scoffed. "The fuck I did. *I* put that deal together myself. I met the CEO at a benefit auction. We got to talking, and I was the one who told him he had a real shot at going public. I put that deal together. I spent months on that thing. It was Ron that swooped in at the eleventh hour and stole all my hard work."

I shook my head. "No. My father only sent me to work

for you to get back what was rightfully his. He told me you'd been doing it to him for years, and he was tired of losing. He told me he had lost millions of dollars because you kept stealing from him."

He shook his head, getting to his feet. I stayed put, watching him jerk on his underwear and pants. "That's not what happened and I think you know it."

"I know what my father told me," I said.

"And you believe him? After everything?"

"I was twenty-one Devin. I didn't know anything else. I had no idea who my father was then."

He laughed incredulously. "But you know now, don't you? And you agreed to come back and help him again."

"I told you that was about protecting my family legacy," I argued, getting angry myself.

He pulled his shirt on, leaving it hanging untucked. "This is such bullshit. We have a chance of moving on. We could be happy together, but I can't tolerate you still having sympathy for your father. Not after everything he's done."

Deep down I knew he was right, but it still didn't sit well that he was trying to tell me who I could be in business with and who I couldn't. And despite all my father's faults, he was still my father. And he was the only parent I had left."

"You won't tolerate it? I'm not a fucking child Devin," I spat.

He looked down at me and shook his head, disappointment and disgust written all over his handsome face. He walked out of the apartment without another word. I couldn't bring myself to get off the floor. I felt like a tornado had just whipped through and turned my world upside down again. We had the strangest, most volatile relationship

I had ever heard of. We were up and down more than a heartbeat.

I slowly pulled myself together and redressed. I hated that things had ended badly after they had gone so well. It had been awesome to watch him with Lizzy. And the way he'd made love to me felt completely different than it had before. It had been sweet and tender.

"Oh Devin, what am I going to do with you?" I whispered.

Now, I had to worry about what he was going to do about Lizzy. I had been able to relax earlier, but now my guard was back up. The desire to flee was strong. I could pack her up and be on the next flight to Los Angeles. I had no doubt he would find me, but it would give me a running start. I would hire an attorney and make sure it was clear my home was in LA. If he wanted a fight, it was going to be on my turf—not New York.

I took a deep breath, steadying my nerves. Panicking wasn't going to help. I would give him some time to cool down. I had to see the deal through. He would be in a better mood and would hopefully be willing to listen to reason.

My father, on the other hand, he was another matter entirely. I needed to have a stern conversation with him. I would not allow myself to be his pawn. I knew his game, and I was done playing it. I had helped him as much as I was going to. If he and Devin went after the same account again, it was between them. I was done trying to referee the two of them.

CHAPTER 25

DEVIN

I couldn't get my head in the game. I had been trying to focus on the new projections for a company I was considering investing in. I had looked at the numbers, and it just wasn't sinking in. I had a serious mental block going on. The only thing my brain wanted to think about was Elly. Elly and Lizzy.

How in the hell was I ever supposed to have a relationship with the mother of my child if she continually sided with her asshole father? I didn't even care about what she had done. I had truly forgiven her for that, but for her to think I was a thief—I couldn't deal with that. I was a lot of things, but I had never stolen a damn thing, especially not from that piece of shit Ron Savage.

I kept repeating her words. *She forgave me.* It was insulting. I didn't do shit. She didn't have to forgive me. I had to let it go. I had to figure out a way to get my head back in the game. I couldn't let her continue to mess with me, or it was going to destroy my business and give me an ulcer.

I shut down the computer and stuffed a couple of files

in my briefcase before walking out of the office. I went home and walked into the sterile, cold, empty town house. I dropped my briefcase on the table next to the door and went to the kitchen to find something to drink.

I opened the fridge and scanned the scant contents. It was empty. Just like the house. Just like my life. I had a taste of what life could be like with Elly and Lizzy, and it left me feeling emptier than I ever had been.

"Fuck this," I said with frustration. I pulled out my phone, made a call, and then headed upstairs to pack a bag. I had to get out of the city. I needed to clear my head and figure out what the hell I was doing with my life.

An hour later, I was in the car heading to the airport where my private jet was waiting to take me to Anderson, Nebraska. I was hoping some time in the cabin on the lake I had purchased would give me some clarity. I needed a sign from God or some other deity. I needed to know whether I should pursue something with Elly or let it go. My head said to do the latter. My heart was urging me to chase her, despite the knife she kept stabbing me with.

"Thank you," I said to the driver I had hired to ferret me from the airport to the cabin. It wasn't exactly a rustic cabin, but it was much smaller than my town house. I carried my suitcase into the main bedroom on the ground floor.

I wasn't sure how long I was staying. I could work from the cabin if there was a pressing matter that had to be handled. My phone rang in the other room. I debated ignoring it, but now that I had a child, I needed contact with the outside world.

It was Wes, which was oddly coincidental that he would be calling shortly after I landed in his hometown. "Hello?"

"Hey! I heard you were in town. Were you planning on saying hi?"

"How in the world did you know I was here?"

He laughed. "This is Anderson. I heard from a friend that works at the airstrip that the McKay jet had landed."

"Damn, that is next-level spy shit," I said with a dry laugh.

"We keep tabs on our town. Can't have a bunch of city slickers invading us."

"I was planning on minding my own business."

"Since you're here, we'd like to invite you to dinner tonight," he said.

I grimaced. "I don't know. I'm not really in a good mood. I don't think you want me around for dinner."

"Sure we do. Just come over. We'll cheer you up."

"Thank you, but maybe tomorrow night," I said.

There was a strange sound followed by Rian's voice coming on the line. "Devin McKay get your butt over here. I'm cooking meatloaf and mashed potatoes. You need a good home-cooked meal, not that slop you get at your fine-dining establishments."

I had to laugh. "Rian, you know how much I love meatloaf," I said. "But—"

"Nope. No buts. Be here at seven. Ronny would love to see you. She has not stopped talking about that magic fish you and Wes caught the last time you guys went fishing."

I rolled my eyes. "You do know that was a fish story, an actual fish story."

"I know that, but Ronny will not listen to reason. She thinks you walk on water and will not believe you didn't catch the biggest fish in the world."

"All right, you are relentless. I'll be there soon."

"See you then," she said and hung up.

It wasn't exactly the lonely night I was prepared for, but maybe it was for the best. It was hard to be sad around Ronny. I finished unpacking before going out to the garage where I kept the new truck I had purchased for my time in Nebraska. I got in and started it up. It was strange to drive. Strange, but good. I was going to have to go for a nice long road trip tomorrow if time allowed.

When I arrived at the Brown household, it was bright and cheery and so full of life. Ronny talked a mile a minute telling me all about her adventures. It was nice to have so much life around me.

"Dinner's ready," Rian called from the kitchen.

"We better get in there, or your dad is going to eat it all," I told Ronny.

She giggled and took off running. I followed behind her and took the seat Ronny insisted I sit in. Dinner was good; the conversation was light and easy. I was glad they had bullied me into coming for dinner. It truly did lift my spirits. Once dinner was over, I helped clear the table, feeling like part of the family.

"I'm going to get Ronny to bed," Rian announced. "I think I'll turn in as well."

Wes gave her a kiss before giving Ronny a kiss on her cheek.

"Good night, ladies," I called out. "Thank you for dinner."

"I'll grab us a couple beers, and we can sit outside and enjoy the peace and quiet. I know you don't get much of that in the city."

"You got that right," I agreed.

We headed out and sat down in the comfortable chairs. It was so quiet. I could see the stars twinkling high above and found myself getting lost in thought. "Here you go," Wes said, handing me a cold beer.

I twisted the top off and took a long drink. "It really is nice here. I think I can see myself doing this one day."

"It's nice. It's an adjustment but taking it easy and enjoying life and all it has to offer is very rewarding."

"Maybe, but you have to have a life to enjoy," I replied.

"So, what's going on? What has you hiding out in Nebraska?"

I took another drink. "A woman I cared about. She's back in my life. She's been keeping a huge secret from me for years."

"Ouch," Wes said.

I realized Wes was the right man to talk to. He out of everyone would understand. "She had my baby and never told me. She never told me she was pregnant."

Wes let out a low whistle. "Been there, done that. It isn't easy. I guess the first step would be to start with why? Why didn't she tell you? Were you in a relationship that went bad?"

I sighed before explaining the whole story to him. He nodded, agreeing it was definitely a difficult situation.

"The most recent fight is because she thinks you stole from her father, right?"

I nodded. "Yes. I didn't steal shit. You know me. Everything I have, I have worked my ass off for."

"She doesn't know you."

"She knows me," I insisted.

"When she went to work for you, it was because her father told her you had been stealing from her. She was a young kid. Of course she's going to believe her father. She obviously feels a sense of loyalty toward him. You said Ron Savage was a first-class asshole. Just try to imagine what it was like to grow up with him filling her head with bullshit. She was probably brainwashed."

I shook my head. "Even if she did believe it then, she should know me better by now. She *does* know me better. If she really believes I'm a liar and a cheat, why in the hell does she keep sleeping with me?"

Wes laughed. "I'm not even going to try and answer that."

"She kept my child from me, yet she thinks I'm a thief. What the hell is that about?"

"Have you talked to her? Rationally. Without tossing around insults and accusations. Both of you need to try and see the problem from one another's point of views. I believe you when you say you're not a thief, but you need to make her believe you. Without getting angry."

"How am I supposed to change her mind?" I asked.

He shrugged. "The truth. I know it sucks, but if she doesn't believe you now, I don't think you're going to be able to change her mind. Then you have to decide if you can get over it. Can you be with a woman who thinks you've been stealing from her father?"

"I don't think so," I answered honestly. "When it comes to her, my judgment is skewed. I always look right past her betrayal and her lies. And without fail, it bites me in the ass every time. I know I shouldn't trust her, but I can't help being drawn back to her. You know those bug zapper things? All those bugs see their buddies getting fried, but they can't stop themselves. They head right into the bright light and get zapped. That's me. I keep getting zapped, and I'm too fucking stupid to stop."

He burst into laughter. "That's one way to look at. Another way is that you recognize there's someone in there worth loving. I guess you have to consider is a little jolt worth it?"

I grinned. "Yes, but in the long run, I don't know if those jolts are worth getting my heart broken. There's also Lizzy to think about. I can't let this thing between us get messy. I don't want our daughter getting caught in the middle of a war."

"That's smart. No matter what happens, the two of you need to stay friendly for the child's sake. Shit, I still can't believe you're a dad."

"Me either. I'm still trying to get my head around it."

"But you forgive her for keeping the fact you fathered a child a secret?" he asked.

I shrugged. "I understand why she did it. Things were pretty rocky between us. I had just lost out on a project that cost me millions. I'm not happy she did what she did, and I am still pissed about it, but I do forgive her."

"Then I think you owe it to both of you to try and figure this all out."

I finished the beer, mulling over what he said. I supposed in the grand scheme of things, her wanting to believe in her father. I'd only known about my daughter for three days and I would give anything for her to see me as the man I wanted to be.

CHAPTER 26

ELLY

I felt like an empty shell. I had got out of bed that morning, showered, dressed, put on my makeup, and kissed Lizzy goodbye before heading out. I was going through the motions and doing my best to pretend everything was okay. I smiled as I walked into the offices of Toby's company.

"Good morning, I'm Elly Savage," I introduced myself to the woman at the reception desk.

"Hi, Miss Savage. The rest of your team is already setting up in the conference room."

"Thank you," I told her and headed in that direction. I liked that she referred to them as my team, even if they weren't. They were Devin's people. Devin was making all this happen. It was about the last thing I needed. I was trying my hardest to pretend he didn't exist. It was about the only way I could function.

Toby was passing out donuts when I walked in. "Elly!" he greeted.

"Hi, Toby. You guys look like you're off to a great start."

He nodded. "We are. Things are rolling along. These guys have got things well in hand."

"I expected nothing less," I said, taking a seat at the table. Devin's team was an extension of him. He wanted perfection. He would expect nothing less.

"This is where we're at now," one of the men said, sliding a folder over to me.

I picked it up and reviewed it. It was so detailed. I could see how much time and energy went into every line item. There were notes scratched in the margins. It was different handwriting, as if it had been passed around with everyone adding their own two cents.

"This is impressive," I said.

"Isn't it?" Toby said, excitement in his voice.

"I'm putting together some numbers for initial projected stock sales with the lower start price," the same man said.

I nodded. "Perfect. I'm going to work on putting together a list of contacts."

"Great."

The room buzzed with various conversations. I focused on making my list, but no matter how hard I tried, I kept thinking about Devin. I hated that things had been going so well between us. I wished I could erase the past, pretend it never happened. Of course, if I did that, I wouldn't have Lizzy.

Why couldn't I have it all? Why couldn't I have Devin the man, the father of my child, without all the baggage? There was so much baggage between us it continually got in the way. We managed to take one step forward and tumbled two steps back. Every time we made headway in our relationship, something came up. That something always revolved around my time working in his office.

He'd become irate when I'd told him what my father

had told me. He had so vehemently denied all of it and he'd looked so sincere in all of it.

Had Had been misled? I felt sick. I got up so fast from the table I knocked over an empty coffee cup. "Sorry," I muttered.

I closed my laptop and rushed out of the conference room. "Where's the ladies' room?" I asked.

The receptionist pointed down a hall. I moved fast. I felt violently ill. I rushed into the bathroom and went into a stall, locking it behind me. I waited to see if I would actually throw up. When I didn't, I walked out of the stall and turned on the cold water.

Everything I thought I knew about me and my dad and the company was called into question. My mind did a mental rewind, going over all the conversations I had ever had with my father pertaining to Devin and the business. I had been going to work with my father for years before I'd even graduated high school. I knew the ins and out of the business, but I had never really seen the financials.

I worked on some deals, but I never had all the pieces. Everything was called into question. Everything I thought I knew about my dad, the business, Devin, everything was suspect. There was only one way to know for sure. I had to confront my father directly.

I soaked a paper towel and used it to dab at my face. After taking a few deep breaths and pulling myself together, I went back to the conference room. I wasn't really needed, and any questions would be direction toward Devin anyway.

"I've got another appointment," I said with a smile on my face. "You guys are doing a great job. Keep it up."

"See you later," Toby said with a wave.

I walked out, doing my best to appear normal. I was

feeling anything but normal. I hailed a cab and headed for my father's office, assuming he still had the offices. When I walked into the building, I checked the directory. I winced when I saw my father's company only had one small suite. In the good old days, there had been two full floors of offices.

"Oh, how the mighty have fallen," I muttered before walking to the elevator and pushing the button.

I stepped out of the elevator and scanned the plaques until I saw the suite number for my dad's office. I opened the door, and although it still had the look of a successful operation, underneath the shiny veneer there were visible cracks.

I looked at the furniture in the waiting area. It was outdated and worn. The carpet, once luxurious, was frayed in the corners. The painting that hung on the wall was an obvious cheap knockoff. I strolled through the doors that once led into a bustling office. It was eerily quiet. I popped my head into the breakroom and found it empty. The coffee maker stood alone on the counter. It didn't look like it had been used in a long time.

I walked to the double doors at the end of the hall and knocked once. "Dad," I called out.

"Come in," I heard him say.

I was almost afraid of what I would see when I opened the doors. I pushed one open and stepped inside. I winced when I took in the emptiness. His office was huge, and he still had his massive desk, but the Van Gogh that had once hung behind him was gone. The Persian rug in the seating area was missing, and in its place was another knockoff. He was trying to hold on to the idea he was rolling money, but the truth was clear. And it was also clear he'd been dozing at his desk. In the middle of the day.

Seeing him sleeping on the job of what had once been a vast empire was sad. The empire was falling to ruin. It was a very apt description of the trajectory of my life as well. If only I had known my entire life had been built on a house of cards.

"What are you doing here?" he asked, not exactly nicely.

"We need to talk," I told him, taking a seat in the worn leather chair.

"You're right, we do," he snapped. "Let's start with you telling me why you sold me out to that slimeball."

I immediately took offense. "I didn't sell you out, but that's not what I need to talk to you about."

"Did he double-cross you? I knew it was a mistake to go into business with him."

"No, he didn't do anything. He's making sure you get rich again. Judging by the look of this place, you need it."

"Watch your mouth, young lady," he growled.

"I need to ask you something," I said, feeling nauseous all over again.

"What is it?" he asked, straightening his tie.

"Three years ago, when you sent me to work for Devin, you told me it was because he stole a deal from you. You wanted me to get it back for you. Did you lie?"

"Did I lie about what?" he asked.

"You told me Devin stole that deal from you. Is that true?"

He wouldn't look at me. "In business, one man might think he owns the rights to something, when in fact, he doesn't necessarily own it."

"That's not an answer," I told him, a sinking feeling in my gut. "Who orchestrated that deal?"

He cleared his throat. "The company had put out

feelers for an investor. I responded and was hoping to secure the deal for us."

"Hoping? You never actually had it?"

He shrugged. "I would have had McKay not jumped in."

I closed my eyes. "You told me it was yours and Devin stole it out from under your nose! You lied to me! You had me go into his office and commit theft of proprietary information! You could have ruined my reputation in the field."

"We needed that cash infusion, Elly. Our company was going under fast. There was a string of bad investments, and we were going to lose everything."

I shook my head. "So, you thought the answer was to take from someone else? Devin secured that deal. He did the work, and you had me steal it all out from under him."

"Obviously he's recovered just fine," he spat.

"That's not the point," I argued. "I did something horrible because you lied to me. You told me horrible things about him and what he supposedly did to you. Was any of it true?"

He shrugged. "Devin is one of those arrogant pricks who thinks his shit doesn't stink. He walks around like he's a god. He deserved to get taken down a peg or two."

My eyes widened. "Why? Because he was more successful than you?"

He slapped his hand on the desk. "Because I was a major player before his father and guys like him came along. They started outbidding me and promising more than I could keep up with. They drove me into the ground!"

I got up and shook my head. "No, Dad. You did that all by yourself."

I walked out, ignoring whatever it was he was trying to say. I had nothing more to say to him. He was a despicable man. He was the liar and the cheat. He was the con man. I couldn't believe I had been so naive to fall for his lies.

I didn't care that he'd lost the family fortune or the family business. I cared that he cost me what I was sure was my one shot at real happiness with Devin. How could I ever expect Devin to trust me? If I were in his shoes, I wouldn't. I wouldn't believe anything that came out of my mouth.

My heart felt heavy as I walked along the sidewalk. Commuters in a hurry to get to wherever they were going jostled me back and forth. I barely felt it. I thought about Lizzy. Her own grandfather had stolen away a little piece of her life because he was a liar. It was so unfair. The sins of the father had certainly been visited upon us.

I couldn't claim complete innocence in the situation. I had willingly gone along with my father's plan to steal information. It didn't matter if I thought I was doing it to get even. Two wrongs didn't make a right. I did owe Devin an apology, and I would have to find a way to tell him. If he would even give me the time of day.

CHAPTER 27

DEVIN

I had been right to get out of town for a day or two. I felt refreshed and ready to tackle the Elly situation head-on. Wes had helped me put some perspective on the situation, and I realized I simply had to be the bigger man. I had to be willing to forgive all and move forward, or I would never get what I wanted.

And I wanted Elly. I wanted her and Lizzy in my life. I knew I was risking my heart, but I had to talk to her. I had to know if she was willing to set aside the baggage that kept bringing us down and move forward with a future I was certain could be very good for both of us.

If she was willing to hear me out, I wanted a promise that we would always be brutally honest with each other from that point on. No more secrets. No more lies. If she was willing to agree to that, we could figure out the rest. I had no doubt in my mind that we had a bond that was unlike anything other people felt. Maybe I was being arrogant, but I was confident what we had was special. I felt it every time we touched. I knew she had to feel it as well.

"I'll need to make a stop at the toy store," I told the driver.

"Yes, sir," he answered, pulling the car to a stop.

"Ten minutes," I said, jumping out and going inside.

I knew exactly what I was looking for. I went directly to the aisle with all the stuffed animals. I smiled when I saw the teddy bears that were damn near as big as I was. Another time. For now, I needed something a bit more subdued. I found a beautiful, silky black bear with pink feet and a pink ribbon. It was perfect.

I paid for the bear, already mentally picking out the other items I would be buying for my little girl once things were settled. I was going to spoil the hell out of her. She was going to be a spoiled little princess, and I didn't give a shit who said otherwise.

"Here," I said when the driver pulled up to Tiffany's.

I caught his smile in the mirror. "Should I wait?"

"Yes, I don't think this will take long."

He chuckled. "You might want to take your time with this purchase."

I grinned. "I already know exactly what I want."

It took me less than thirty minutes to make my purchase. When I got back into the car, I gave him Elly's address. I was nervous as hell. I had no idea if she would even agree to see me. I wasn't even sure she was in town. Part of me had worried she would hop a plane and leave the city again.

"Can you please let Elly Savage know Devin McKay is here to see her?" I asked the doorman.

He gave me a look that made me wonder if he knew about our relationship. "Just a moment."

He walked to his small desk and picked up the phone. I waited, holding the cloth bag in my hand. If she refused to see me, I would have to get creative. I wasn't going away until I got her to talk to me. I needed her to hear me out. I could hear the doorman speaking in a low voice, his back to me. I was beginning to lose hope when he turned to me and nodded. "You can go up."

"Thank you," I breathed with a sigh of relief.

I practically ran to the elevator, tapping my foot as it slowly climbed the floors. I wiped my sweaty palms on my legs, waiting for the elevator doors to open. I made my way down the hall and stared at the door. I hadn't exactly rehearsed what I would say, but I wanted to make sure I said as much as I could before she booted me out.

When she opened the door, all worries about her being angry with me faded. "Elly?" I asked, noticing the red puffy eyes and the telltale signs that she'd been crying.

"What do you want, Devin?" she asked. Her voice was filled with resignation as if she expected me to kick her while she was down.

"Can I come in?" I asked, worried to ask about why she was crying. She sighed and held open the door. "Fine."

The moment I was through the door, Lizzy ran to me, carrying the unicorn. She wrapped her arms around my legs, giving me her version of a hug. My heart practically melted. "Hi, Lizzy," I said, patting her head. I couldn't move out of fear I would knock her over.

"Let's go play," Lizzy said.

Lizzy let go of my legs and headed into the living room. Elly handed her a sippy cup and settled her in on a blanket spread out on the floor. A strange cartoon was on that quickly captivated Lizzy's attention.

"Are you okay?" I asked Elly in a low voice.

"I'm fine," she answered without conviction. "Have a seat."

I sat down on the couch, my eyes going to Lizzy, who was stacking LEGOs together and watching TV at the same time.

"Why are you here?" she asked.

"I was hoping we could talk about a few things," I told her.

"I don't want to fight with you anymore. I really just don't have it in me."

"I don't want to fight anymore either. I've had some time to think about things, and I know I absolutely want you and Lizzy in my life. I've realized I don't want to lose you. Either of you."

She let out a big sigh. "This yo-yo thing is too hard. I hate the ups and downs. The ups are greats, but the downs are really awful."

I nodded. "I agree. I don't want to fight. It does us no good. I'd like to try and work through our issues and move on from them."

"Is that even possible?" she asked. "You have some pretty strong feelings about things. I'm not saying I blame you, but I can't change what's already done."

"I know. I don't want to rehash all that. I want us to be open and honest from this point on. I want the two of us to figure out a relationship."

She didn't look convinced. "What does that even look like?"

"I don't know. I was hoping we could work that out together."

She wrinkled her nose. "Why would you want to bother? We always bring each other so much frustration."

I smiled. "I think that frustration means we care. We wouldn't get so aggravated if we didn't care."

She smiled. "I suppose that's true."

"I can still remember the first time I laid eyes on you. You were a fresh-faced intern fresh out of college and ready to conquer the world. I saw those baby blues, and I was smitten. When I'm thinking about you and some of the stuff we've been through, I think of you as my kryptonite."

She laughed, a soft tinkling sound. "Kryptonite? Is that supposed to be a compliment?"

I shrugged. "Yes and no. You have the power to cripple me. I can brush anyone else off, but with you, I care. I care about what you think of me. I want to be a man you can want to be with. I want to be good enough for you, for her."

"You are good enough. It's me who has the flaws."

"I have wanted you from the very moment I saw you," I told her. "I told myself I couldn't have you, but it didn't stop me from wanting you. That night in my office was one of the best nights in my life. I knew then I wanted to be with you."

She scoffed. "Until you found out who I was."

"Honestly, even after everything came out, I still wanted you. The last three years I've dreamed about you every night. I haven't been with another woman since you. There is no other woman who compares to you. You are the gold standard in my eyes. You are the one I want to be with. Our differences are there, and we do have some stuff to work out, but it will be worth it."

She didn't look convinced. "There's so much baggage. How can we ever really get over that?"

"We will if we try. I know we can be good together. We can be good for each other."

"I don't know," she said, chewing on her lower lip. Her eyes moved to our daughter happily playing. "Look at me," she said, turning her eyes back to me. "I'm a mess. I can't be like this. It isn't good for her to see me like this."

"I don't want you to be sad," I told her, fighting the urge to touch her. "I'll do everything in my power to keep you from being sad."

She rubbed a hand over her face. "This is not what I was expecting."

"Good. I like to keep you guessing."

"I like when things are good between us," she finally said.

"Then it's settled," I said, slapping a hand on my thigh. "We'll make things good between us."

"As if it's that easy," she groaned.

"It isn't easy, but we have to try. It isn't just us we have to think about." I looked at Lizzy and smiled. "She needs her parents to be happy. It would be great if we could be happy together and give her the life she deserves. No matter what, I'm here to stay. I'm not abandoning either of you."

She was quiet for several seconds. I felt like I was losing her in that moment. Panic welled inside me. I had to do something and fast. I couldn't lose her.

"Elly, I'm sorry. I treated you harshly. I shouldn't have. I let my own hurt get the best of me. I shouldn't have spoken to you the way I did. No matter what transpired between us, you didn't deserve to be disrespected that way."

"Please, don't apologize," she whispered.

My heart pounded in my chest. I sensed she was about to tell me it was too little, too late. I didn't know what else to say or do to make her understand I could be the man she needed. I could take care of her and Lizzy. I would always treat them well.

"Wait," I said. "Don't make a decision right now. Please, think about it. I know things are still a little raw from our last fight. Don't decide when you're obviously still upset about that. Please, give it a day, two, whatever it takes. I'll wait. I'm not going anywhere. If you go back to California, I'll follow you. I need you, Elly. I don't know how else to say it. I need you and our daughter in my life."

Her hands were in her lap, nervously twisting. I thought about getting up and leaving before she could say whatever it was she was trying to put together. If I didn't hear her shoot me down, that meant I still had a chance as far as I was concerned.

"I'll go." I jumped to my feet. "I'll call you tomorrow and we can talk then."

"Devin, wait," she said, stopping me from my hasty exit. "Please, sit. There's something I need to say."

I sighed and flopped back down. I felt defeated. Whatever came next would change my life either way. I told myself I shouldn't be surprised. I had known I was taking a huge chance by showing up at her door. Maybe I was a closet hopeless romantic. I was hoping a big gesture would change everything. I hadn't even gotten the chance to make my grand gesture. She was shutting me down before I could get started.

CHAPTER 28

ELLY

The man had poured his heart out, so it was only fair I come totally clean. He said he wanted total transparency moving forward. I agreed. The only way a relationship would ever work was if we were completely open and honest with one another.

"Devin, there's something I have to tell you. I don't know where to start."

His eyes were filled with sadness. He was such an amazing man. For him to forgive me for everything said a great deal about the man he was. A tear slid down my cheek. I wanted all that he said. I wanted the relationship and the life together, but I didn't feel worthy.

"Elly, I'm sorry," he croaked out the words. "Please, give me a chance to prove to you I can be a good man."

"Devin, that's not it. I know you're a good man. It's me who is unworthy."

"No!" he blurted out. "You are perfect."

"I'm not," I said, unable to meet his eyes. "I talked to my

father. I asked him about what happened three years ago. You were right."

He looked confused. "About what?"

I reached out and grabbed his hand. "About everything. I swear to you I didn't know."

"Know what, Elly?" he asked, his demeanor changing. "What? What happened?"

"My dad lied to me. He told me that deal was his and you used some underhanded double-dealing to get if from him. That's what he told me back then. He said it wasn't the first time and that you and your father had set out to ruin him. He was on the verge of going under. I believed him. When he asked me to get into your firm and steal it back, I didn't hesitate. I should have. I should have questioned his motives."

"Elly, I believe you," he said.

"I never would have done that if I had known the truth. That isn't an excuse, though. What I did was wrong. I should have asked more questions instead of blindly believing what he said. A good person would have found another way. A good person wouldn't have resorted to deception and thievery."

He pulled me close to him, wrapping an arm around me. "You are a good person, which is why you did what you did. You were trying to help your father. You were being a loyal daughter. I admire that. I look at you and I can see how great of a mother you are."

I wanted to believe his words, but my own guilt was plugging my ears, rejecting his kindness. "I'm so sorry. I hate what I did. I feel so much guilt it's almost unbearable."

"Elly, don't feel guilty. I mean it when I say it's over. It's forgotten. I want to move forward. Don't think about it ever again."

I wished it were that easy. "I'll try, but how will you ever be able to trust me? You said it before—I've betrayed you, lied to you, deceived you."

He smiled and shrugged a shoulder. "I do trust you which is why I have no problem telling you I love you."

I froze, my eyes going big. "I love you too," I replied. I couldn't believe he had said the very words I had been holding back from him. "I've loved you from the first time I walked into your office. I was the starry-eyed intern hot for the boss. I remember looking at you and trying to see what my father saw in you. I saw a patient man with a knack for the business. Not to mention you are pretty easy on the eyes."

He laughed. "You're not so bad yourself."

"For what it's worth, there's been no one else but you since that night. I fell madly in love with you, and I wanted no one else but you. Even when I was confident I would never see you again, it didn't matter. I didn't want another man. I only wanted you."

"I'm very glad to know that," he said, releasing me and turning to grab the bag he had dropped on the floor. "Lizzy, come here," he called.

I smiled, suspecting he had brought her another gift. She was hard not to spoil. Lizzy walked right to him. "This is for you," he said, holding out the bag.

Lizzy grinned. "Present?"

Devin nodded. "Yes, a present." He pulled at the drawstrings holding the bag closed and left it wide open for her. I watched as she pulled out a new teddy bear.

"Lizzy, what do you say," I prompted.

"Thank you," she said, loving on the bear.

"Lizzy, show Mommy the box," he said, pointing to the pink box in the bear's hands.

I looked at him, wondering what he was up to. It took a little convincing to get Lizzy to surrender the bear to me while I opened the box. "Oh my God," I gasped when I saw the ring inside. I looked to Devin with tears in my eyes. "Devin?"

"Elly, I know this is completely unconventional, but I know there is no other woman for me. You are the only woman I want. I want to spend the rest of my life with you and Lizzy. I want to build a beautiful family with you. I want to wake up next to you every morning and put our daughter to bed together every night. I want banana pancakes on lazy Sunday mornings and all the birthdays and holidays we can have. Will you marry me?"

My heart was filled with so much love it felt like it would burst. "Yes," I breathed the word.

He pulled the ring out of the box and slid it on my finger. I stared down at the massive diamond surrounded by gorgeous blue stones. It was stunning and far more than I could have ever dreamed of.

"Do you like it?" he asked. "We can get something different if it isn't your style."

"Devin, it's gorgeous! Look at Mommy's ring, Lizzy. Look what Daddy got for Mommy!"

Lizzy looked at Devin and offered him a toothy grin. I doubted she understood the word daddy, but it was a word she was going to learn.

"Daddy." Devin almost choked on the word. "That's a word I never thought I would hear."

I offered a watery laugh. "Trust me, once she picks up on it, you'll probably wish she wouldn't have."

"Never. I don't think I will ever get tired of hearing her call me Daddy." I watched as he picked her up, pulling her into his lap. "Do you like your new teddy bear, Lizzy?"

"I like," she said with a smile. "Thank you."

"You're very welcome," he answered, giving her a big hug before kissing the top of her head.

Together, we watched another of one Lizzy's shows before I decided an early bedtime was a good idea. I wanted to be alone with my fiancée. "Lizzy, it's time to get your jammies on," I said.

Devin looked at me, silently asking the question. "Stay," I whispered.

He nodded. "I will."

Together, we got Lizzy ready for bed. He loved helping her brush her teeth. It was the cutest thing ever. I thought about taking a picture but then decided there would be plenty more opportunities in the coming months and years.

"Story," Lizzy insisted.

"I can do it," Devin quickly volunteered.

"Okay," I said, having something else I wanted to do while he was with her.

I left the room and quickly stripped the bed in my father's room before putting on new sheets. I wanted to sleep beside him for the first time. He found me just after I had put on fresh pillowcases.

"What's going on here?" he asked.

I smiled, shrugging a shoulder. "My dad hasn't slept here once. I figure we may as well sleep comfortably."

He chuckled. "Sleep is about the last thing I have on my mind."

I giggled. "Me too."

He pulled me against him and passionately kissed me. I held him close, kissing him back and letting all the feelings I had been trying to fight for so long bubble to the service.

"I love you," he whispered, trailing kisses over my jaw

and down my neck. "I will always love you. You are mine forever and always."

His words sent gooseflesh spreading over my skin. They were words I had longed to hear for too many years. "I love you," I told him as he pulled my shirt over my head.

We frantically undressed before climbing into the freshly made bed. A bed. I couldn't wait to try something very traditional with my untraditional man in our absolutely untraditional relationship.

"I'm taking my sweet time with you tonight," he said, going up on one elbow and looking down at me. "In a bed. No desk, no hard, slippery floor, and no cramped couch. I hope you don't have any plans for tomorrow."

"Tomorrow?" I breathed, my body tuned into every word he was saying.

"You're going to be up late," he answered with a kiss on my breast.

"Oh," I softly cried out. "I'm used to no sleep."

"Good," he murmured against my flesh. The vibration of his voice against my skin sent shivers up and down my spine.

He began a trail of kisses that started at my shoulders and ended at the tips of my toes. Every sense, every nerve ending, every cell in my body was tuned into him and what he was doing to my body. I twitched and spasmed under his touch.

When he began the trail of kisses back up my body, I was convinced I had stumbled through the pearly gates and found myself in a heavenly place. Never had I felt so good. "I've wanted to do this for a long time," he whispered, his mouth hovering over my belly button.

I looked down at him, taking in the sight of his dark

head of hair perched over my stomach. "We've done this," I said with a small smile.

His eyes met mine. "Not this," he answered before sliding back down my body and nudging my legs open.

When his mouth covered the apex between my legs, I nearly screamed. I caught myself at the very last second and clapped my hand over my mouth. My hips bucked as his tongue lapped over my clit. "Oh God," I groaned. The overwhelming feelings of ecstasy were doing something to my body I couldn't explain.

He lapped over me, his tongue parting my folds and finding its way inside my very core. My hands went to his hair, pulling and pushing as I struggled to find some semblance of control. My body was putty in his capable hands. I trusted him. I gave myself over to him, and the reward was an orgasm that nearly had my eardrums popping and my head feeling like it was going to explode.

"Devin." I said his name on a breath as my body went through something absolutely amazing.

He kissed a trail of kisses up my belly until his naked body was over mine. His fingertips brushed back the strands of hair clinging to my face. "You okay?" he gently asked.

I moaned. "I'm so okay. That was amazing."

I kissed him and shoved his left shoulder. He was knocked off balance and fell to the mattress. I pushed him onto his back and sat beside him. I stared down at the body of the man I was madly in love with.

"Elly, I need you. We can do that another time."

I frowned at him. "I don't think so. Fair is fair."

He chuckled. "Then by all means, have your way with me."

I traced a fingertip over one defined pectoral muscle

and then the next. "I plan on it." I leaned down and dropped a kiss on his hard chest. "Devin?"

"What is it, baby?" he asked on a breath. The sound of his tender voice was sweet music to my ears.

"How do you stay in such good shape?"

His throaty laugh tickled the nerves that were still feeling like little live wires all over my body. "Swimming. A lot of swimming. It turns out, you left me a very frustrated, horny man, and swimming was the only thing that helped take the edge off."

I kissed over his washboard abs. "So, what you're saying is I'm responsible for this?"

He grunted when I reached my hand down and cupped his heavy balls. "Yes."

"Good."

CHAPTER 29

DEVIN

Her hot mouth was driving me to the point of insanity. I was barely hanging on to consciousness. My self-control was pushed to a new level of strength. My fists dug into the sheets stretched over the bed as her head bobbed up and down on my dick. Never, ever in my entire life had I been made to feel so good.

"Elly," I said on a groan. "Baby, please, you're turning me inside out."

Her tongue lapped over the head of my cock, damn near sending my body flying into the ceiling. I wasn't sure I would survive very long if I was going to have her in my bed every night. I would die of ecstasy. She would give me an ecstasy overdose.

Her hot mouth pulled away from me, her tongue slicing over my stomach as she made her way up my body. I reached for her, desperation making me crazy. My hands went to her hips. I lifted her and dropped her on my dick. If I didn't bury myself inside in her, I was going to lose my fucking mind.

I could feel her slick heat glide over me. "I need you," she breathed.

I looked up at the woman looking down on me. It was the sweetest, most erotic sight I had ever seen. I reached up to cup her cheek in my hand. "You have me. You will always have me. I am never leaving you, and I will fight like hell if you try to leave me."

Her eyes were filled with such love it hurt. My heart was beyond full. I knew I would spend the rest of my life in love with her. No matter what happened, no matter the fights we were likely to have or the hardships that came our way, I would always love her.

She positioned her body with her opening hovering over the head of my cock before she slid down the length. Our eyes were locked together as our bodies joined. It wasn't just a physical joining. In that moment, I could feel our souls fusing together. We would always be together.

She released a long, contented sigh as her body engulfed mine. "God it's so good," she breathed.

My hands stroked up and down her thighs. "It is beyond good."

She began to move, a slow leisurely ride on my dick as she teased and titillated both of us. Her hips rocked and rolled and did a slow grind that nearly had me blowing my wad before I was ready. Her hands pressed flat against my chest as she moved faster. Her breasts bounced, teasing and just out of reach.

"Oh God," she moaned, her back arching and her head dropping back as she slid her hips forward and back.

"Don't stop," I ordered. My body was wound so tight my eyes felt crooked. I couldn't see straight.

She moaned, reaching up and squeezing her own breasts. The erotic sight was more than my taxed self-control could take. She was completely lost in the passion. Her body was glowing as she chased her orgasm, taking me along for the best ride of my life.

I held on to her hips, feeling the explosive orgasm brewing. I didn't want to buck her off when it hit. The power I felt building inside me was a little alarming. I let go of the control I had barely been wielding and gave over to what she was doing to me.

I shouted once before remembering the sleeping little girl across the hall. My hips bucked forward, and as expected, I nearly sent her flying into the wall headfirst. I held her down, her body joining mine in a violent, twisting orgasm that had us both groaning and moaning.

She collapsed against my chest, her tight pussy milking the last drops of ecstasy from me with each spasm. I wrapped my arms around her and held her close to my body. Our hearts pounded against one another. Our breathing was fast and ragged.

"Wow," she murmured against my chest.

"Yes, wow."

She slid to my side. I kept my arm around her, holding her close to my chest. I was damn well going to cuddle with her. I wasn't letting her go. Ever.

In that moment, I felt like a whole man. I felt like everything was exactly as it should be. It wasn't a feeling I had ever had before. There was a sense of inner peace that made me feel like I was home, truly home.

"I knew you were the woman for me," I said.

She turned her face to look up at me. "How could you possibly know that with all the drama we went through?"

I smiled. "Because you never give up on anything. You are a tenacious woman, and when I recognized not only your brilliant mind, but your sense of duty and loyalty, I knew I wanted you."

"You're crazy!" she giggled. "We have been in a three-year fight."

"Not at all. It was a misunderstanding. I wish we would have talked three years ago, but I'm happy with the way things have turned out. We had to go through all that to get where we are. We had to fight to be together, and I think that will make us fight a lot harder when we have arguments in the future."

"Are you planning on arguing with me?"

"You're a strong-willed person, and so am I. We're both passionate about what we like and don't like. There are bound to be some disruptions from time to time."

She turned and kissed my chest. "I guess it isn't just opposites that attract."

"Nope. I think the thing I admire about you the most is when you are faced with a problem, you push through. You don't give up, you get creative."

"You are the same way. You didn't give up on us."

I squeezed her closer to me. "I couldn't if I wanted to. There was something about you from the first moment we met that had me hooked."

She let out a long sigh. "I never stopped thinking about you. I would be sitting on a beach in California and dreaming about a life that included you. I cannot tell you how many times I wished I could go back in time and change what happened."

"Elly, you have to let it go. I've heard the saying everything happens for a reason. I believe it. We went through all that so we could get here. I don't think either of us could have accepted a happy ever after without going through some trouble first."

She laughed. "I suppose, but seriously, three years? I think that's a bit excessive."

"It's three years we have to make up for."

Her fingers were tracing a little circles over my chest. "I wish there was a way we could forget all about what happened in the boardroom and keep our focus on the bedroom. With my father, I have a feeling that problem is going to keep rising up."

"No, it won't. Your father is not my problem. He isn't your problem. I have been running my business just fine without him. I'm not going to think about him. I won't begrudge you for your relationship with him, but I don't see me inviting him over for dinner. Not yet."

She groaned. "Trust me, I don't think I'll be inviting him over anytime soon. Not that he would want to. He used me and I think he will always use me given the chance. I'm not going to be his pawn. I tried to help him. I tried and tried and tried. I can't help him."

"He has to want the help, and he has to stop doing what he's doing," I said. I was not interested in discussing her father while we lay naked in bed together. Ron Savage was not wanted in my bedroom or anywhere else.

"I'm sorry," she said. "I won't bring it up."

"I don't want you to disown your father or anything like that. I want to be with you, and I know that includes him. Just don't plan on happy get-togethers for a while."

"I got it."

We lay quietly a while longer. I was already planning our future. I had a family now. That thought boggled my mind. I'd been a single bachelor convinced I would spend the rest of my days alone, and now I had a woman and a child. It was a lot to take in.

I had never been happier in my life. I couldn't help but

look back on the lonely nights and the stark feeling of being empty and alone and wonder if it had been the journey I needed to get me to where I was just then. I had to fight to get Elly, and I wasn't sure I would have fought so hard if my life had been different. I had to go through that hell to learn I never wanted to be back there and that she was worth fighting for.

"I'm never letting you go," I told her.

"That's a good thing because I don't plan on leaving. I'm not sure what the future holds for us, but I want it all. I want the good and the bad. This is real for me. I know in my heart you're it for me. There will never be another."

He words filled my heart with joy. "Me too. I will follow you to the ends of the earth. If we fight, promise you will stay and yell at me. Tell me what I've done. Give me a chance to fix it. No more secrets—ever."

She leaned up and dropped a kiss on my lips. "I promise, no more secrets."

"So, does this mean we're going to be business partners now?" I teased.

She giggled. "I don't know how much business would actually get done if we were working together."

I laughed. "I don't mind trying. Mixing a little pleasure with business keeps things interesting."

"We'll have to see about that," she said, sliding back onto my chest.

I put my hands on her face, staring into those dangerous blue eyes that had hooked me from the very beginning. "I'm willing to do whatever. Work with me. Don't work at all. Hell, if you want to start your own business, I'm okay with that. My only request is you, me, and our little girl are together."

"I think I can make that promise," she whispered.

Her mouth closed over mine, sealing the promise with a kiss I would never forget. I knew we had something unbreakable. It would likely be tested, but it would never be broken. Both of us were too damn stubborn to let anything get in the way of what we wanted. I was confident she wanted me, and I knew with every fiber in my being that I wanted her.

We were in it for the long run. No one, not even Fion Savage, would ever come between us.

EPILOGUE

ELLY - SIX MONTHS LATER

I stood in front of the full-length mirror inside the massive closet Devin and I shared. It was an important day, and I wanted to look good. I turned left, then right, checking my reflection in the mirror. It was a new outfit courtesy of my adoring fiancé.

I straightened the black Armani blazer. The cropped pants and the black pumps were perfect for the warm spring weather. I felt powerful. I felt like a woman at the top of her game. I stepped closer to the mirror and fluffed my hair before settling on the look.

I headed downstairs, dropped a kiss on Lizzy's head, and promised to see her soon before joining Devin in the waiting car out front. "You look amazing," he said, leaning over to give me a kiss.

"Thank you. I feel confident."

"You should be. This is a big day, and you are going to kick some serious stockbroker ass."

I laughed. "I'm not kicking any asses—unless nobody buys the stock. Then there will be some ass kicking."

I sat back and enjoyed the ride down to Wall Street. I wasn't nervous. Not really. I had Devin by my side, and that gave me all the confidence I needed. We were ushered inside and talked with a few people before we were escorted to where I would be ringing the bell to start the trading day.

"You ready for this?" Devin whispered next to my ear.

"I'm so ready. This has been months in the making. Toby's company is about to go public, and we did that. I can't believe this day is finally here."

He was smiling at me, looking at me with a great deal of pride. I waited until I was given the signal before I rang the bell, kicking off the first day of trading on Toby's stock. Toby, Devin, and I stood back and waited, intently watching the screens.

"There!" Devin pointed.

We all looked, watching Toby's stock get bought up, trading higher than expected. Toby grabbed me and pulled me into his arms. "Thank you." He shook Devin's hand. "Thank you both so much. This is huge."

"You're welcome," I told him.

"I can't believe I'm standing here watching this happen," he said with genuine surprise. "I've waited so long, and to watch a dream become reality, it's just, I have no words."

I smiled at him. "I think I can understand a little Thank you for giving me the opportunity to work with you on this. It's a big deal, and I'm so glad I got to be a part of it."

"I should probably get to the office," he said, his cheeks flush with his excitement. "I promised the team we would celebrate."

"Take care and we'll be in touch," Devin said.

Devin reached for my hand, holding it in his as we watched the action on the floor. I had never been to the

New York Stock Exchange. It was wild and chaotic and confirmed I never wanted to be a broker. We watched for a good thirty minutes, both of us enthralled with the way the business worked.

"Why don't we slip away for a minute," he said next to my ear.

I looked up at him and grinned. "Bathroom?"

He laughed. "Come on now, I've got a little more class than that."

I gave him a dry look. "It was last week when we had sex in the bathroom of the airport."

He shrugged. "I didn't want to wait until we got on my jet."

I laughed, letting him pull me away from the chaos. The man was insatiable. Then again, I was just as insatiable. We argued we had three years to make up for and had been going at each other for the last six months, unable to get enough of one another.

He pulled me into a small office and closed the door behind us before practically jumping on me. His mouth was hot and demanding, his hands roaming over my body in a heated make-out session.

"This outfit is really doing it for me," he breathed before finally taking a step away from me.

"You like the power suit thing?" I laughed. "Most men like skimpy maid outfits or sexy cheerleader and you like business suit?"

He shrugged. "I like a confident woman that is smart and powerful. You really, really turn me on, and yes, I want you to wear that to bed tonight."

I laughed, shaking my head. "You're crazy."

"Crazy in love with you."

He lunged for me again but not before I caught the

hungry look in his eye. "Devin, we can't," I hissed, pushing away from him. "We're going to get caught."

He groaned. "Let's go home."

"Relax, big boy," I told him, straightening the jacket and trying to fix my hair.

"I'm so proud of you," he said with a smile. "You are amazing. You worked your ass off, and it's paying off tenfold."

"I could not have done any of this without you. You made this possible."

He slowly shook his head. "Nope, this is your firm. I only helped in the beginning, but this is all you."

I couldn't help the smile that spread over my face. "My firm. I still can't believe it's mine. Finally."

"Your dad can't stand that you're smarter and more successful. His retirement is the best thing for all of us. Honestly, I can almost stand the guy now that he's officially retired."

I laughed. "Me too. I still have so much work to do to get that firm back up to where it was, but I'm confident it will happen. With Toby's stock prices already shooting up, it's looking very possible."

"I'm sure Ron will be calling you any minute," Devin said. "He's probably sitting on some Florida beach with his phone in hand watching the stock. He's going to want his piece of the pie."

I shrugged. "I don't mind giving him his share as long as he keeps his ass in Florida. I told him I would make sure he was taken care of as long as he left the business to me. I talked with him yesterday and let him know what was happening today. For the first time ever, he thanked me."

"Thanked you for saving him from a life of destitution?" he quipped.

"No, thanked me for pushing him out. He said he hated the business. He hated the grind and the money managing and all of it. He only took over the business because his father essentially made him do it. He told me he was proud of me."

Devin's jaw dropped. "He what?"

I smiled and nodded. "Yep. He said he was happy I took over and he was proud of the talent I had, and he wished he would have walked away sooner. And he apologized for everything in the past."

"Wow. I don't even know what to say to that."

"Me either. I'm still processing it all. I'm hoping it's a step in the right direction for all of us. I'm hoping one day we can have one of those family gatherings you are so against."

He grimaced. "If he doesn't mention money or politics, I would be willing to have him over."

She smiled. "Good, because I've invited him to Christmas this year."

He groaned. "It's far enough away, I'll have some time to get my head around that idea."

"Exactly."

He reached for me again, putting his hands on my waist. "So, what's the first thing you're going to do with all the millions you're going to make today?"

I gave him a coy smile. "The first thing I'm going to do is redecorate the guest room on the second floor."

He raised an eyebrow. "Why? Don't tell me for your father. We're a long way from him moving in with us."

I slowly shook my head. "Not for my father. I need to transform it into a nursery."

Several lines appeared along his forehead. "A nursery?" he questioned with confusion. "What's a—" he stopped talking. His eyes widened. "Are you saying we can think about having another baby?"

I laughed. "I'm saying, there is no thinking about having another baby."

"What?"

"I'm pregnant," I told him.

He pulled me in, hugging me tight and spinning me around before releasing me and letting out a loud hoot. "I knocked you up again!"

I burst into laughter. "You sound pretty proud of yourself."

"Damn straight I am. A baby. Holy shit. I cannot wait to see you round with my baby growing inside you. I'm going to spoil you. I'm going to buy you everything you crave, no matter if it's at three in the morning. I'm going to rub your feet and carry you everywhere. I'll have the elevator fixed. You can't be navigating those stairs."

"Slow down," I told him, seeing the excitement taking over. "I'll be fine taking the stairs."

"Lizzy's going to be a big sister," he gasped. "Another baby. Two babies! I want to fill the house with our babies."

I put my hand on his chest. "We'll talk about that later. Let's get through this one first."

He bobbed his head up and down before putting his hand against my stomach. "When? When do I get to meet my next child?"

"I'm thinking around Christmas."

"Oh. That's not much time. I've got so much to do."

"Devin, you just said it was far away," I reminded him.

"That was before I knew we were having a baby. You're right, we need to do the nursery. We need to babyproof the house. Maybe we should buy a new house in the country."

I grabbed his face with my hands and soundly kissed

him, slowing him down. I felt him relax as he gave over to my kiss. "We'll talk about all of that later. We do have time."

He slowly nodded. "Okay."

"You good?"

"I'm so much better than good. I didn't know I could ever be this good. I'm so happy. Is it even possibly to be this happy?"

"You're rambling again," I told him.

He grabbed my hand and pulled me out of the office, heading straight for the doors. "Where are we going?" I asked him.

"Hotel," he answered.

"Why are we going to a hotel?" I asked with confusion.

"Because I want you, and you don't want me to take you in the bathroom. We can't go home with the nanny and Lizzy. I don't want to go to my office or your office. We're getting a room."

I giggled, shaking my head. The man was spontaneous. I loved that he didn't let anything stop him from getting what he wanted. I loved that I was what he wanted. I had a feeling if our lust for one another didn't slow down soon, I would find myself in a constant state of being pregnant.

We walked into an upscale hotel where Devin quickly paid for a room. No one questioned why we didn't have luggage. Once inside the room, he showed me just how happy he was to know he was going to be a father for a second time. As we lay together in the bed, holding each other close, I thought about my life. I was looking forward to spending the rest of my days with him, raising a family and surrounding them with love.

"I love you," I said, the words actually making me choke up a little.

"I love you. I will always love you. But Elly, there's something I need to say."

My head jerked around to meet his eyes. "What?" I snapped.

"You have to marry me and fast. We've been waiting until after the deal closes. It's closed. I don't care if we go down to the courthouse or fly to Vegas, but I want to make this official. I want it all."

I grinned. "What's your schedule like next week?"

He chuckled. "I'm yours. Always and forever, I'm yours."